Hell.

He could still tast
temptation to take
near overwhelming.

Cody looked down into her dazed, upturned face.
His breathing had yet to return to normal. "If you're
waiting for me to say I'm sorry, you've got a long
wait ahead of you," he warned.

Catherine moved her head from side to side—
slowly so as not to fall over. "I don't want you to
say you're sorry," she whispered.

"Good," he finally declared. He pulled his Stetson
down farther until the brim all but obscured his
eyebrows and hid his eyes. "'Cause I don't know
why the hell I just did that, but I know I'm not sorry
that I did," he emphasized.

And then, just like that, Cody turned on his heel and
went back to his vehicle.

Dear Reader,

Welcome back to Thunder Canyon, Montana, and the fine citizens of that town who make life there so very interesting. Last time, I got to write about Calista Clifton, one of eight brothers and sisters (perhaps you see a pattern here?). This time around, my book centers on Catherine Clifton's story. Catherine is the oldest girl and has always been the caretaker in the family (my lord, can I relate to *that*), sublimating her own needs and dreams in order to care for everyone else. Well, now just this one time, it's her turn to get something. Jasper Fowler's neglected antiques store had closed its doors and was up for grabs. Summoning her courage, Catherine took the plunge, buying it with the intention of turning it into not just a place where forgotten antiques were kept to gather dust, but a shop where vintage clothing and intriguing one-of-a-kind items were sold. Catherine was looking for customers. She certainly wasn't looking for a man to win her heart, but she got both in Cody Overton, a genuine cowboy who was still grieving for his late wife eight years after he'd lost her.

This is a story about two lonely, independent and self-sufficient people who found each other and accidentally wound up filling the void in the other's life. I hope you like it.

As always, I thank you for reading my book, and from the bottom of my heart I wish you someone to love who loves you back.

Marie Ferrarella

REAL VINTAGE MAVERICK

MARIE FERRARELLA

HARLEQUIN®
entertain, enrich, inspire™

Special thanks and acknowledgment to Marie Ferrarella
for her contribution to the
Montana Mavericks: Back in the Saddle continuity.

Recycling programs
for this product may
not exist in your area.

ISBN-13: 978-0-373-65692-9

REAL VINTAGE MAVERICK

www.Harlequin.com

Printed in U.S.A.

MARIE FERRARELLA

This *USA TODAY* bestselling and RITA® Award-winning author has written more than two hundred books for Harlequin Books and Silhouette Books, some under the name Marie Nicole. Her romances are beloved by fans worldwide. Visit her website, www.marieferrarella.com.

To
Stella Bagwell,
who is strong enough
to actually live the life
I can only write about

Prologue

The sound of her laughter filled his head as well as his heart, echoing all through him. Generating within him, as it always did, a feeling of tremendous joy and well-being.

It was one of those absolutely perfect Montana mornings that begged to be pressed between the pages of his memory. Cody Overton tried to absorb it as much as possible, instinctively knowing that it was important he do so.

Very important.

He and Renee were at the state fair—Renee always loved the state fair—and, as always, the love of his life had coaxed him onto one of the gaily-painted horses on the weathered carousel while she had mounted the one right next to it.

"Tame stuff," Cody had pretended to grumble before they got on—as if he ever could have denied Renee anything. "At least let's ride the Ferris wheel instead."

But Renee paid no attention to his protest. His wife absolutely *loved* riding the carousel; she always had, even when they'd been in elementary school together. He'd teased her that he was surprised she hadn't insisted on their taking their wedding vows sitting astride two of the horses on the carousel.

Renee had laughed and said that they would have had to wait for the state fair to come through and she hadn't wanted to delay becoming Mrs. Cody Overton a moment longer than she had to.

She had always had a sense of urgency about living life to the fullest. It never made any sense to him.

Until, sadly, it did.

"Maybe, if we close our eyes and wish real hard, the carousel'll go faster. C'mon, Cody, give it a try. Close your eyes and wish," she'd entreated, wrapping her hands around the horse's pole before her. She was like a ray of sunshine. "Don't you believe in wishes?"

Not anymore.

The words seemed to silently resonant in his head even as the carousel began to speed up, spinning faster and faster. Just as she'd wished it would.

And as the speed increased, so did the sound of her laughter, until that was all there was, just her laughter overpowering everything else.

And all the while, they were spinning ever faster and faster.

Cody kept trying to see her, to fix his eyes only on his beautiful Renee, but suddenly, he couldn't find her, couldn't see her.

Couldn't see anything at all except a sea of smeared color bleeding into itself.

She was gone.

Twenty-five years old and she was gone.

His soul realized it before his mind did.

He began calling out her name, but nothing came out of his mouth except for an anguished, guttural cry.

With a start, Cody bolted upright in his bed. As always, when this dream came to him, he was covered in sweat and shaking.

The crisp September weather had slipped into the bedroom, thanks to a window he'd forgotten to close, but he was still sweating.

Still shaking.

Still praying it really wasn't just a dream. That Renee was still alive and with him.

Nurturing a hope that was completely foreign to his very practical, pessimistic outlook, Cody slowly looked to his left, to the spot beside him that had once belonged to Renee.

Aching so badly to see her that it physically hurt. But he didn't see her. She wasn't there, as he knew she wouldn't be.

She hadn't been there for eight years.

Hadn't been *anywhere* for eight years because she'd been dead for eight years. Another statistic to the ravages of the insatiable cancer monster.

His heart had been dead just as long.

At times, Cody was surprised that it was still beating, still keeping the shell that surrounded it alive and moving.

A man with nothing to live for shouldn't be required to live, Cody thought darkly.

He tossed off the covers and got out of bed despite the darkness that still enveloped the room. He knew it was useless to try to go back to sleep. Sleep was gone for the remainder of the night. If he was lucky, a glimmer of it might return by that evening.

Most likely not.

Slipping on the discarded jeans he picked up from the floor, Cody padded across the bare floor to the window and looked out.

There was nothing to see, just a vastness that spread out before him.

His ranch.

Their ranch.

"Why did you leave me?" he demanded in angry frustration, not for the first time. "Why did you have to go?"

He wasn't being reasonable, but he didn't much feel like being reasonable. It wasn't fair that he had been left behind, to face each day without Renee after she had filled so much of his life before then. He couldn't remember a time when he hadn't known her, hadn't been aware of her. The very first memory he had was of her.

Eight years and he still wasn't used to it. Hadn't made his peace with it. Eight years and a part of him still expected to see her walk through the door, or see her standing over the stove, lamenting that she'd burned dinner—again.

He'd never minded those burnt offerings—that was what he'd teasingly called them, her burnt offerings—and he would have been willing to eat nothing else for the rest of his life if only he could see her one more time. Hold her one more time...

He supposed, in a way, that was what the dreams were about. Seeing her one more time. Because they were so very vivid that, just for a moment, Renee was alive again. Alive and the cornerstone of his world.

He wished he could sleep forever, but that wasn't going to happen.

Cody dragged his hand through his hair and sighed. He might as well get dressed and get started with his day, even if it was still the middle of the night. The ranch wasn't going to run itself.

"I miss you, Renee."

His whisper echoed about the empty bedroom just as it did about his empty soul.

Chapter One

It happened too quickly for him to even think about it.

One minute, in a moment of exasperated desperation—because he hadn't yet bought a gift for Caroline's birthday—Cody found himself walking into the refurbished antique store that had, up until a few months ago, been called The Tattered Saddle.

The next minute, he was hurrying across the room and managed—just in time—to catch the young woman who was tumbling off a ladder.

Before he knew it, his arms were filled with the soft curves of the same young woman.

She smelled of lavender and vanilla, nudging forth a sliver of a memory he couldn't quite catch hold of.

That was the way Cody remembered it when he later looked back on the way his life had taken a dramatic turn toward the better that fateful morning.

When he'd initially walked by the store's show window, Cody had automatically looked in. The shop appeared to be in a state of semi-chaos, but it still looked a great deal more promising than when that crazy old coot Jasper Fowler ran it.

Cody vaguely recalled hearing that the man hadn't really been interested in making any sort of a go of the shop. The whole place had actually just been a front for a money-laundering enterprise. At any rate, the antique shop had been shut down and boarded up in January, relegated to collecting even more dust than it had displayed when its doors had been open to the public.

What had caught his eye was the notice Under new ownership in the window and the store's name—The Tattered Saddle—had been crossed out. But at the moment, there was no new name to take its place. He had wondered if that was an oversight or a ploy to draw curious customers into the shop.

Well, if it was under new ownership, maybe that meant that there was new old merchandise to choose from. And that, in turn, might enable him to find something for his sister here. As he recalled, Caroline was into old things. Things that other people thought of as junk and wanted to discard, his sister saw potential and promise in.

At least it was worth a shot, Cody told himself. He had tried the doorknob and found that it gave under his hand. Turning it, he had walked in.

Glancing around, his eyes were instantly drawn to the tall, willowy figure on the other side of the room. She was wearing a long, denim-colored skirt and her shirt was more or less the same color. The young woman was precariously perched on the top step of a ladder that appeared to be none too steady.

What actually caught his attention was not that she looked like an accident waiting to happen as she stretched her taut frame out, trying to reach something that was on a higher shelf, but that with her long, straight brown hair hanging loose about her back and shoulders, for just an instant, she reminded him of Renee.

A feeling of déjà vu seized him and for a moment, his breath caught in his throat.

Balancing herself on tiptoes, Catherine Clifton, the former Tattered Saddle's determined new owner, automatically turned around when she heard the little bell over the front door ring. She hadn't anticipated any customers coming in until the store's grand reopening. That wasn't for a couple more days at the very least. Most likely a couple of weeks. And only if she could come up with a new name for the place.

"We're not open for business yet," Catherine called out.

The next thing out of her mouth was an involuntary shriek because she'd lost her footing on the ladder and both she and the ladder were heading for a collision with the wooden floor.

The ladder landed with a clatter.

Catherine, fortunately, did not.

She was saved from what could have been a very bruising fate by the very person she'd just politely banished from the premises.

Landing in the cowboy's strong, capable arms knocked the air out of her and, along with it, anything else she might have said at that moment.

Which was just as well because she would have hated coming across like some blithering idiot. But right now, not a single coherent thought completed itself in her head. It was filled with just scattered words and a myriad of sensations.

Hot sensations.

Everything had faded into the background and Catherine was instantly and acutely aware of the man whose arms she'd landed in. The broad-shouldered, green-eyed, sandy-haired cowboy held her as if she weighed no more than a small child. The muscles on his bare arms didn't even appear to be straining.

A tingling sensation danced through Catherine's entire body, which was stubbornly heating up despite all of her attempts to bank the sensation—and her reaction to the man—down.

Her valiant efforts to the contrary, for just a moment, it felt as if time had stood still, freezing this moment as it simultaneously bathed her in a heretofore never experienced, all but debilitating, feeling of desire. For two cents proper, using the excuse that this rugged-looking cowboy had saved her, she would have kissed him. With feeling.

Catherine could absolutely visualize herself kissing him.

The fact that he was a complete stranger was neither here nor there as far as she was concerned. Desire, she discovered at that moment, didn't have to make sense. It could thrive very well without even so much as a lick of sense to it.

And for no particular reason at all, it occurred to her that this man looked like the real deal. A cowboy. A real vintage cowboy.

Was he? Or had she managed to bump her head without knowing it and was just hallucinating?

Their eyes met and held for a timeless instance. Only the pounding of Catherine's heart finally managed to sufficiently rouse her.

"Thank you," she finally whispered.

Doing his best to focus and gather his exceedingly scattered wits about him, Cody heard himself asking, "For what?"

Catherine let out a long, shaky breath before answering. "For catching me."

"Oh." Of course that was what she meant. What did he think she meant? Cody nodded his head. "Yeah. Right."

The words emerged one at a time, each containing a sealed thought. Thoughts he couldn't begin to convey, or even understand.

Cody cleared his throat, then realized that he was still holding the woman in his arms. He should have already released her.

Feeling awkward—he hadn't spontaneously reacted to a woman in this manner since his wife had died—he set her down. "Sorry about that."

"Don't be," she told him. "I'm not." *I'm not sorry at all.* "If you hadn't caught me just then, I might have broken something—either some of the merchandise or, worse, one of my bones."

The fact that if he hadn't come in just now, her attention wouldn't have been thrown off and she very well could have remained perched on the ladder was a point Catherine had no desire to bring up. Thinking of him as her hero was far more pleasant.

Rather than comment, the tall cowboy merely nodded his head in acknowledgment. At the same time, he began to back away.

"Didn't mean to trespass," he murmured by way of an apology. He reached behind him for the doorknob, ready to make his getaway.

"You're not trespassing," Catherine was quick to protest. She didn't have the heart to chase out someone who could actually *buy* something in the store. "It's just that I haven't exactly gotten the store ready for customers yet. But you can stay if you like."

If he didn't know better, he would have sworn that her tone was almost urging him to stay. And she had shifted her body so that she was now standing between him and the front door.

Cody glanced around the store, still mulling over her initial protest. "Looks okay to me," he told her. "Actually, it looks a mite better than it used to look when that old guy owned it."

Catherine was eager to bring out the shop's better features and play them up so that she could attract actual customers rather than just the pitying or dismissive glances that the store had been garnering before she'd bought it. After the former owner had kidnapped Rose Traub, the people in Thunder Canyon had deliberately shunned the store. And from what she'd heard, before then the clientele was almost as ancient as some of the antiques that were housed here. She wanted to change that as well. She wanted all age-groups to have a reason to drop by and browse.

Fowler wasn't in the picture anymore, having been sent to prison, and the shop was something that she wanted to take on as a project, something that belonged to her exclusively. After a lifetime of being the go-to person, the main caregiver in a family of eight and always putting everyone else's needs ahead her own, it occurred to Catherine that time—and life—was slipping by her. She needed to make her own way before she woke up one morning to discover that she was no longer young, no longer able to grab her slice of the pie that life had to offer.

Since this sexy-looking cowboy seemed familiar with the way the store had been before she'd taken over, Catherine made a natural assumption and asked, "Did you come in here often when Mr. Fowler owned it?"

"No," he told her honestly. Antiques had never held any interest for him. And they still didn't, except that he knew his sister liked them. "But I walked by the store whenever I was in town and I'd look in."

Mild curiosity was responsible for that. He might not look it, but Cody had made a point of always taking in all of his surroundings. It kept him from being caught off guard—the way he had when Renee had become ill.

"Oh," Catherine murmured. All right, the place had held no real attraction for him, at least it hadn't before. But he'd walked in this morning. Something had obviously changed. "Well, what made you come in today?"

She glanced over her shoulder to see if there was anything unusual out on display that might have caught the cowboy's eye. But nothing stood out for her.

Cody wasn't sure what this gregarious woman was fishing for, but he could only tell her the truth. "I'm looking for a present for my sister. Her birthday's coming up and I need to get something into the mail soon if it's going to get there in time."

Okay, she wasn't making herself clear, Catherine thought. Desperate to hone in on a reliable "X-Factor," she tried again.

"Why here?" she pressed. "Why didn't you just go

to the mall? There're lots of stores there." And heaven knew a far more eclectic collection of things for someone to choose from.

The expression that fleetingly passed over the cowboy's tanned face told her exactly what he thought of malls.

But when he finally spoke, he employed a measured, thoughtful cadence. "I haven't put much thought into it," he readily admitted. "I guess I came here because I wanted to give Caroline something that's genuine, that isn't mass-produced. Something that isn't in every store from New York City to Los Angeles," Cody explained.

He looked around the shop again, but not before discovering that it took a bit of effort to tear his eyes away from the shop's new owner. Close up, the talkative young woman didn't really look like Renee, but there was an essence, a spark, an unnamable *something* about her that did remind him of his late wife. So much so that even as he told himself that he really should be leaving, he found himself continuing to linger on the premises.

"The stuff in this store is…" His voice trailed off for a moment as he searched for the right word. It took a little doing. For the most part, Cody Overton was a man given to doing, not talking.

Catherine cocked her head, waiting for him to finish his sentence. When he didn't, she supplied a word for him. "Old?"

"Real," he finally said, feeling the word more aptly described what he was looking for. "And yeah, old," he agreed after a beat. "But there's nothing wrong with old as long as it's not falling apart," he was quick to clarify.

Catherine smiled. She liked his philosophy. In a way, it embodied her own.

And then, just like that, an idea came to her.

Her eyes brightened as she looked up at the cowboy that fate had sent her way. This could be one of those happy accidents people were always talking about, she thought.

But first, she needed to backtrack a little. "I'm sorry, I completely forgot my manners. My name's Catherine Clifton," she told him, putting her hand out. "I'm the new owner," she added needlessly.

Cody looked down at her hand for a moment, as if he was rather uncertain whether to take it or not. He wasn't a man who went out of his way to meet people. Even an extremely attractive woman. He kept to himself for the most part.

But again, there was something about this woman that pulled at him. That nudged him. After a beat, he slipped his hand over hers.

"Cody Overton." He felt it only right to tell her his name since she had given him hers.

He watched in mute fascination as the smile began in her eyes, then feathered down to her lips. "Pleased to meet you, Cody Overton," she said. "You're my very first customer."

"Haven't bought anything yet," he felt obligated to point out.

The man was obviously a stickler for the truth, she couldn't help thinking. She liked that. Moreover, she could really use someone like that, someone who would tell her the truth no matter what.

She paused a moment, wondering how the man would react to what she was about to propose.

Nothing ventured, nothing gained, right?

Catherine felt good about this. The sparkle in her deep, chocolate-colored eyes grew as she dove in. "Cody, how old are you?" she wanted to know.

The question caught him completely off guard. The last time he recalled being asked his age like that, he'd been a teenager, picking up a six-pack of beer for his buddy and himself. At the time, he'd figured that his deep voice and his height would make questioning unnecessary. He'd assumed wrong.

He fixed the young woman with a look, wondering what she was up to. "If you're planning on asking customers their age, once word about that gets out, I don't think you're going to have too many of the ladies coming in." And everyone knew that it was women, not men, who liked this old furniture and knickknacks.

"I don't care how old *they* are," Catherine protested. "I mean, I do, but I don't—" She stopped abruptly, realizing that she was getting tongue-tied again. Taking a breath, she backtracked. "I'm trying to appeal to a certain dynamic—a certain age-group," she corrected herself, not wanting this rugged cowboy to think she was trying to talk over his head. But what she'd just said didn't sound quite right, either. "Let me start over," she requested. Taking a deep breath, she paused for a second before plunging in again. "What I want to do is attract a certain age-group—younger than the people who used to come into the store—so I thought if I could maybe pick your brain once in a while, find out what you think of some of the merchandise, it might help me improve sales once I open."

If possible, the woman was making even less sense to him than before.

Hell, if she was trying to find out what would attract guys like him, all she had to do was look in the mirror, Cody couldn't help thinking. Because, confusing though she seemed to be every time she opened her mouth, this new shop owner was a damn sight easy on the eyes. If she stood in the doorway—or near her show window—that would definitely be enough to bring men in on the pretext of shopping.

But, curious to see if there was something more to what she was suggesting, Cody asked, "Why would you want to pick my brain?" His taste was plain and, if it were up to him, he wouldn't have set foot in here in the first place.

In answering his question, Catherine didn't go with the obvious: that there was something compellingly fascinating about this vintage cowboy who had strolled into her shop just in time to keep her from breaking something vital. Instead, she gave him something they could both live with.

"Because what you like is what would appeal to other people in your age bracket."

He'd never thought of himself as being like everyone else. Not that he saw himself as unique, just…different. The gadgets out there that held such fascination for men—if he was to believe the occasional commercial he saw—held no interest for him. He was a man of the earth, a plain, simple man who'd never felt the need to be part of the crowd or to join anything at all for that matter.

With a shrug, he finally got around to answering the initial question she'd put to him. "I'm thirty-five."

That was about where she would have put him, Catherine thought, feeling triumphant.

"Perfect," she declared out loud, stopping short of clapping her hands together. "You're exactly what I'm looking for. Business-wise," she quickly qualified in case he got the wrong impression. She didn't want him thinking she was staking him out for some reason. The last thing she wanted was to chase this cowboy away.

Cody looked at the exuberant woman for a long moment. He sincerely doubted that he was the type that *any* woman was looking for, at least not anymore. There was a time when he would have been. A time when he'd been eager to plunge into life, to be the best husband, the best father he could possibly be. A time when he greeted each day with hope, thinking of all that lay ahead of him and Renee.

But all that had changed once Renee had died. Whatever he'd had to offer in terms of a normal relationship had died and had been buried along with his wife.

He was tempted to tell her she was wrong in selecting him, but he could see that there was just no putting this woman off. She had a fire lit under her, and if he wasn't careful, that fire could burn them both.

Still, he supposed he had nothing to lose by going along with her in this. She'd undoubtedly find his answers boring, but until she did, he could view this as a distraction. God knew he was always looking for something to distract him. Something to block his dark thoughts so that he didn't have to dwell on just how empty his existence had become and continued to be.

Eight years and nothing had changed. He was still just going through the motions of living, placing one foot in front of the other.

"I don't know about perfect," he finally said to Catherine with a self-deprecating laugh that sounded as if it had come rumbling straight out of his chest, bypassing his throat, "but if I can help—" he shrugged "—sure."

If possible, her eyes brightened even more. It made him think of the way a satisfying, steaming cup of hot coffee tasted on a cold winter's day.

"Really?" Catherine pressed, this time actually clapping her hands together as if he was some magical genie who had just bestowed the gift of three wishes on her.

Cody shrugged again in response to her question. "Why not?" he said even as a part of him whispered a warning that he had just taken his first step on a very narrow ledge. A step that could result in his tumbling down into an uncharted abyss at a moment's notice.

All things considered, he supposed that there could be worse things.

Chapter Two

"So exactly how is this going to work?" Cody asked her after a beat. As a rule, he wasn't a curious man, but in this case, he had to admit that this woman had managed to arouse what little curiosity he did possess. "Are you going to be showing me pictures of the stuff you're thinking of selling at the store, or what?" Before she could answer the question, Cody felt it only fair to inform her of something. "Think you should know right from the start that I'm really not too keen on broken-down old furniture."

As far as he was concerned, furniture didn't have to be fancy, but it had to be functional—and not look as if it belonged in some garbage heap.

Catherine laughed. "That's good, because neither am I."

She was still feeling her way around as to the kind of focus she wanted to bring to the shop. Right now, she was pretty much making it up as she went along.

Catherine wondered if admitting that to this down-to-earth cowboy would be a mistake. Would it make him think less of her? Or would he just dismiss her present indecision as a "woman thing"? An inconsequential whim on her part? She realized that it would bother her if he did.

His expression registered mild surprise. Cody looked around at the showroom. Everything here was way older than he was. If it wasn't for the fact that Caroline had a weakness for this kind of thing, he would have just called it all "junk" and dismissed the whole place out of hand.

If this woman was really being on the level with him and felt the same way he did, that brought up another question. "Then what are you doing with this store?"

"Changing its image," Catherine answered without hesitation.

How was she going to do that with the things she had to work with? "To what?" he wanted to know.

"To a shop that sells vintage items, whether it's clothing, books, furnishings, whatever." It was a slight matter of semantics she supposed, but there was still a difference.

One she was apparently going to have to explain because Cody moved back his Stetson with his thumb and squinted at the merchandise in the immediate area. "Just what's the difference between something being an 'antique' and being classified as 'vintage'?"

That was easy enough, Catherine thought.

"Price mostly," she answered with a grin that he had to admit—if only to himself—he found rather engaging.

Cody rolled her words over in his head, then nodded. He was willing to accept that. But there was something else.

"Still haven't answered my first question," he pointed out. When she raised an eyebrow, silently asking to be reminded, he said, "What do you want with me?"

I could think of ten things right off the bat, Catherine thought in reply. But out loud she simply said, "I intend to use you for market research."

Cody laughed shortly. "Only market I know is the one I go to buy my supply of eggs, milk and bread."

That was *not* the kind of market she meant. "Think bigger," Catherine coaxed.

"Okay," he said gamely. "How about if I throw in a chicken, too?"

Obviously this wasn't going to be as simple as she'd hoped. "I'm talking about the general buying market out there," she explained. "You're just the age bracket I'm trying to attract."

Cody's eyes met hers. "You ask me, you keep on smiling like that and you'll attract more than your share of men my age—and older."

The remark pleased her, amused her and embarrassed her all at the same time. Not only that, but she could feel her cheeks growing hot. From the way he looked at her, she knew it wasn't just an internal thing or her imagination. Her cheeks were turning pink. She had an uneasy feeling that her new "researcher" could see the color creeping up into them.

Great, now he probably thought of her as some naive, innocent little girl playing at being a store owner.

"I'm not looking for attention," she told him with feeling. "What I'm looking for are paying customers who are interested in buying what they see."

The way he looked at her told Catherine that she was only making matters worse by talking. But she wanted him to take her seriously, to understand that all she was after at the moment was a business arrangement and a little input from him.

She cleared her throat. "There has to be something that you want—to buy," she tacked on when she realized that she was still sinking into the grave she had verbally dug for herself. She tried one more time, taking it from the top. "When you walked in here, what were you hoping to find?"

"Like I said, I was looking for something for my sister." As usual, he had put getting something for her off, telling himself he had plenty of time until he suddenly didn't.

"Such as?" she coaxed, trying to get him to give her something to work with.

The broad shoulders rose and fell again as Cody shrugged carelessly. "I figured I'd know it when I saw it."

She could accept that. Shoppers didn't always have a clear picture of what they were looking for. "Then look around," Catherine urged, gesturing around the store. "See if anything appeals to you."

She'd been the former Tattered Saddle's legal owner—using her life savings as a down payment— for almost a month now. During that entire time, she'd spent her days clearing away cobwebs, cleaning up and trying to put what she had gotten—the items in the store were included in the price whether she liked them or not—in some sort of manageable order.

To be honest, there was a lot here that she was tempted just to toss out, but she decided that she should seriously consider calling in an expert to appraise everything before she began throwing things out wholesale. However, experts cost money. Someone like Cody Overton did not and it was to the Cody Overtons that she intended to sell.

See if anything appeals to you.

Cody looked at her for a long moment as her words echoed in his head. And then the corners of his mouth curved—just a little. Had this been years ago, he thought, he would have been tempted to say that what appealed to him was her.

But that was a remark for a young man to make, not a man whose soul felt ancient—as ancient as some of the things in this little shop of hers, if not more so.

"Okay," he finally said, moving toward a newly cleaned shelf that displayed a few miscellaneous, mismatched items.

At the very end of the shelf was a small, cream-colored, fringed coin purse. Looking closer, Cody could see that it had been carefully cleaned up so that there wasn't even a speck of dirt or telltale grime on it. In addition, it had been lovingly polished with some sort of leather cleaner. He could tell by the trace of scent on it.

The coin purse felt soft to the touch.

Caroline had always liked things with fringes on them, he recalled. She'd had a vest with fringes on it that their mother had given her when she was a little girl. The vest was a little large for her, but Caroline didn't care. She wore it with everything until it completely fell apart.

There was no price tag visible on the purse, or on any of the other items on the shelf for that matter. Catherine must have just gotten started arranging the things, he reasoned.

Turning around, he held up the coin purse for Catherine to see. "How much you want for this?"

Catherine smiled, secretly relieved that he hadn't chosen one of the more expensive items. "Consider it a gift."

That was exactly what he considered it to be. A gift. The gift he was going to give his sister. "That's what I plan to do with it," he confirmed. Then he repeated, "How much is it?"

Rather than continue standing some distance away, Catherine crossed over to him. Maybe he'd understand her better if she was closer, she thought.

"No, I mean consider it my gift to you in exchange for your services. I can't really afford to pay you yet, but you can have whatever you want in the shop in trade for your help."

Cody was surprised. He hadn't assumed that this woman was going to pay him anything at all. After all, if he understood what she had proposed earlier, this enthusiastic woman was just going to be asking his opinion about things. Didn't seem right asking for money for giving his opinion.

It wasn't as if he was anybody special.

He felt a little guilty about accepting the purse, but then he had a hunch that she was determined to give him something for his services.

"Thanks. This'll do just fine," he told her. "My sister'll like it."

Pleased to have gotten that out of the way—she hated feeling indebted for anything—Catherine put her hand out for the purse. When he looked at her quizzically, she explained, "I'll wrap it up for you."

He was about to tell her there was no need, but then he decided against it. It seemed to make this woman happy to go through the motions of playing shopkeeper and, besides, he was really bad when it came to wrapping gifts.

So he surrendered the purse to her and watched as Catherine placed his sister's gift into a box that just barely accommodated the purse. The fringes spilled out over the side. She carefully folded them into the box until they all but covered up the purse.

"This'll make a nice gift," she told him. Catherine glanced up at him, thinking he might like to hear the story that went with the purse. "It's actually over forty years old. The original owner had it with her when she went to Woodstock."

Reaching beneath the counter, she pulled out a roll of wrapping paper she'd just placed there last night. With what appeared to be a trained eye, she cut exactly the right length of paper for the box.

Completely switching topics, she asked Cody, "Younger or older?"

That had come utterly out of the blue, catching him by surprise. He had no idea what she as asking him. "Excuse me?"

She glanced up at him just for a moment as she clarified her question. "Is your sister younger or older than you?"

"Oh." Why did she want to know that? It had nothing to do with wrapping the gift. "Younger."

Catherine nodded as she took in the information.

The questions didn't stop there. Why didn't that surprise him? "Are you two close?"

"I guess." But that wasn't exactly the real truth, so Cody amended his statement. "We were, once. But then she got married and her husband made her move away—to another state." Caroline's husband had done it to control his sister, Cody was sure of it. The man wanted to isolate and control her so that he could be the center of Caroline's world.

Catherine immediately picked up on his tone. It spoke volumes even if the actual man didn't. "You don't like him much, do you?"

Cody shrugged off the observation, then was surprised to hear himself saying, "Not much to like." He stopped abruptly and looked at this woman who seemed to coax things out of him so effortlessly. "What's with all these questions?" He wanted to know. "This part of your marketing thing?"

Catherine smiled as she put the finishing touches on the box by tying a big red bow on it. "This is part of my getting to know you 'thing,'" she corrected. Then, so he didn't feel as if she was dragging information out of him without giving some up herself, Catherine said, "There's eight of us in my family. I guess I'm just curious about how other people get along with their siblings." She raised her eyes to his, a look of apology in them. "Sorry if I sounded as if I was prying."

Because he couldn't think of anything else to do, Cody shrugged to show her that he hadn't taken any offense at the questions. "Guess there's no harm in asking questions," he allowed. And then he rolled over in his head what she'd told him. "Eight of you, huh?"

"Eight of us," she confirmed.

"They all like you?" If they were, it must have been one hell of a noisy household.

She wasn't exactly sure what Cody was asking her. "You mean are they all girls? No, I've got brothers *and* sisters."

But he shook his head. "No, I meant are they all *like* you," Cody repeated, then, because she was still looking at him quizzically, he clarified, "You know, all enthusiastic and excited, coming on like a house afire."

She'd never thought of herself as particularly enthusiastic, or excitable for that matter. Certainly not in the terms that he'd just mentioned. Shaking her head, she told him, "I'm actually the shy, retiring one in the family."

He laughed at that. It was a deep, all-encompassing sound that made Catherine smile rather than cause her to get her back up.

"Sure you are," he said, adding, "good one" under his breath as he commented on her sense of humor. After a moment, the smile on his lips faded just a little as he looked at her more closely. "Oh, you're serious." Cody took a minute to reassess his opinion. "You all must have been one hell of a handful for your parents to deal with."

"Actually, I was the one who did a lot of the 'dealing with,'" she corrected. "I'm the second-oldest in the family." He probably didn't even want to know that, she guessed.

She was talking too much, Catherine thought. She had a tendency not to know when to stop talking. That was probably one of the reasons she'd decided to buy Fowler's old store. Customers meant that there would be people for her to talk with, even if they left the shop without buying anything.

She liked the idea of meeting new people. Of getting to know things about them.

Catherine looked down at the box she'd just finished wrapping, remembering what Cody had said about the purse's final destination.

"If you're mailing this, I can see if I can find another box to put it in for you," she offered.

She was certainly going out of her way here, Cody thought, especially since he hadn't paid for the purse. On top of that, until a few minutes ago, the overenergized woman hadn't known him from Adam. That made her a pretty rare individual in his book.

"Are you always this accommodating?" he wanted to know.

She couldn't gauge by his expression whether he thought that was a good thing or a bad thing. Either way, she still felt the same about it.

"Nothing wrong with being friendly," she said, flashing a wide smile at him. "Or helpful."

"Didn't say there was," he pointed out. "Just not used to it, that's all."

Fair enough, Catherine thought. She pushed the gaily wrapped gift a little closer toward him on the counter. "So, about that bigger box, do you want it?" she wanted to know.

He was planning on mailing the gift once he left the shop. He supposed that having Catherine provide a box to ship the gift in would be exceedingly helpful in moving things along.

"Sure, I could use it," he allowed. Then he mumbled, "Thanks."

Her smile was triumphant. "You're welcome." And then she couldn't help adding, "There, that wasn't so hard now, was it?" she asked. Because she saw the furrow that had formed across his forehead that indicated to her that he was trying to understand what she was referring to, Catherine clued him in. "Saying thank you," she explained. "That wasn't so hard, right?"

Rather than answer her question, or say *anything* in response, Catherine saw that Cody was looking down at her left hand. Was he checking her out or about to say something flippant about her single status?

In either case, she decided to beat him to the punch. "No, I'm not married."

Cody nodded as if he had expected nothing else. "That explains it."

This time it was her turn to be confused. "Explains what?"

"Explains why you're showering me with all these questions," Cody told her. Then, because she apparently didn't understand what he was telling her, he elaborated, "You don't have anyone to talk to."

She felt a little sorry for the man. He obviously hadn't had the kind of upbringing and family life that she'd experienced. And, to some extent, was still experiencing.

"Oh, I've got people to talk to," she assured him. "Lots of people."

"Then what's with all the questions?" he wanted to know.

"I'm just a naturally curious person," Catherine explained.

Was Cody trying to tell her something? He didn't strike her as a man who worried about being perceived as subtle. If there *was* something that bothered him, she had a feeling he'd tell her.

Maybe not, a little voice in her head whispered. She'd better clear things up now, if that was the case.

"If that's going to be a problem…"

She let her voice trail off so that he could put his own interpretation to what she was driving at.

"No, no problem," he told her. "But it's going to take some getting used to if you're going to be 'picking my brain.'" He used her words to describe their working arrangement.

"You can always tell me to back off," Catherine pointed out.

He was mildly surprised at what she's just said. "And if I do, you'll listen?"

Her eyes seemed to sparkle as they laughed at him. Cody found himself captivated. It took him a moment to retreat from the reaction.

"We'll see" was all she could honestly tell him.

But it *was* an honest reaction and a man couldn't ask for more than that, Cody thought. Honesty was a rare commodity.

"There you go," she pronounced, placing the package wrapped up for shipping on the counter before him. "All ready to be mailed out."

Cody nodded his head in approval as he regarded the box.

"Thanks." He picked it up, then paused for a moment. "I guess I'll be seeing you."

"I certainly hope so." And then she bit her lower lip. Did that sound more enthusiastic than she meant it to? Catherine looked at his face for some sign that she'd made him wary, or worse, and her prime target was going to change his mind and back away.

"How's an hour in the morning every other day sound? Or whenever you can spare the time?" she quickly added.

"Whenever I can spare the time," he echoed, touching two fingers to the brim of his black Stetson just before he walked out of the shop.

Catherine watched him walk down the street through the bay window she'd cleaned that morning. She had a very good feeling about this alliance she'd just struck up.

She smiled, well pleased. Getting back to work, she started humming to herself.

Chapter Three

The need to replenish some supplies in his walk-in pantry brought Cody back into Thunder Canyon a scant two days later.

At least, that was the excuse he gave himself and the two hands he had working for him on his ranch.

The younger of the two ranch hands—Kurt—knowing how much his reclusive boss disliked having to go into town, offered to run the errand for him.

To the surprise of both men, Cody declined, saying something to the effect that he wasn't exactly sure just what he wanted to get. It was a comment that for the most part seemed completely out of character for Cody, a man who *always* knew exactly what he did or didn't want at any given moment.

But the ranch hands knew better than to question their boss, so they merely nodded and got back to cleaning out the horse stalls.

Driving in, Cody took the long way around, passing by the former Tattered Saddle to see how it—and its new owner—was coming along.

The first thing that he noticed was that there was a new sign leaning against the wall just to the right of the front door. From its precarious position, he figured it was obviously waiting to be mounted.

Making a spur-of-the-moment decision, Cody parked his truck close by. Then he got out and crossed to the store to get a better look at the sign as if it was the most natural thing in the world for him to do. The fact that he ordinarily didn't possess a drop of curiosity about *anything* didn't even occur to him or make him wonder at his own behavior.

So, she'd finally settled on a new name, he thought, looking at the freshly painted sign. Real Vintage Cowboy. It was all in tall capitals and printed in eye-catching silver paint.

Cody rolled the name over in his head a couple of times, then nodded to himself. If nothing else, it was a definite improvement over the store's previous name. He'd never quite understood why anyone would want a "tattered" saddle anyway.

Telling himself it was time to get a move on, Cody wound up remaining just where he was. He glanced up and looked through the bay window into the showroom rather than moving back to his truck.

Inside, Catherine was cleaning up a storm, just as she had been doing for the last two days. Although her sisters had initially offered to pitch in and help, she'd stubbornly turned them down. This was something that she was determined to manage on her own.

This way, whatever happened, success or failure, it would be hers alone.

But there were times—such as now when every bone in her body seemed to be protesting that it had been worked too hard—that she felt that perhaps she'd been a wee bit too hasty in summarily turning down her sisters' offer that way.

So when she saw Cody looking in, her heart all but leaped up in celebration. The cavalry had been sighted. Now all that was needed was to pull it in.

Wiping her hands on the back of the jeans she'd decided were more fitting to the work she was doing than the long flowing skirts that she favored, Catherine hurried to the door and quickly pulled it open.

"Hi!" she greeted him with no small measure of enthusiasm, beaming at Cody. "C'mon in," she urged with feeling.

Not waiting for him to make up his mind or to— heaven forbid—turn her invitation down, Catherine grabbed hold of his wrist with both hands and pulled him into the shop. She quickly shut the door behind him in case he was having second thoughts about their arrangement and wanted to leave.

Turning toward the shop behind her, she waved her free hand about. "It's beginning to shape up, don't you think?"

Cody looked around. To be completely honest, he was rather vague about exactly what the place had looked like two days ago, but he could see that she had painted the walls a rather soothing light blue. He assumed that she had done it because he saw a few light blue splotches of paint on her jeans.

Cody slowly nodded his approval, mainly for her benefit. His mother had taught him not to hurt people's feelings if he could possibly avoid doing it, and Catherine seemed rather eager to hear a positive reaction. That being the case, it cost him nothing to give it.

"Looks good from where I'm standing," he told her. Glancing down, he could see that she'd buffed the wooden floors as well. Had she been at this nonstop these last two days?

Well, at least the woman wasn't afraid of getting her hands dirty, he mused.

Taking a quick look around, he saw the back of the sign through the window. He brightened because at least there was something he could actually comment on. "Saw the sign outside. Is that the new name you picked out for the store?"

"You mean Real Vintage Cowboy?" she asked to make sure he wasn't referring to anything else.

When he nodded, Cody saw a strange, unfathomable smile curving her mouth. It piqued his dormant curiosity to some extent.

It piqued a little more when she told him, "Well, you're actually responsible for that."

The furrow above his nose deepened as he sought to understand what Catherine had just said. He was certain he hadn't suggested a name like that to her. He hadn't suggested any name at all that he could remember. She had to have him confused with someone else.

"Me?" Cody said incredulously, staring at her. "I don't understand. How?"

Again, he found the way the corners of her mouth curved intriguing—and completely captivating. "That was what I thought you looked like. A vintage cowboy. The more I thought about it, the more I began to think that it sounded like a good name for the store. So you inspired the name," she concluded brightly. "I guess you could say you're my muse."

"What the hell is a muse?" Cody wanted to know. He thought of himself as a plain man, given to speaking plainly. This sounded like some kind of double-talk to him.

She took no offense at his tone, although she would have thought that he'd be flattered. But then, there was no second-guessing men. Growing up with her bothers had taught her that.

"A muse is something or someone who inspires another person creatively," she told him.

He was having a hard time making the connection. He looked around the store and shook his head. It didn't make any sense to him.

"And I make you think of dusty old junk that people want to get rid of?" Cody asked her, not sure whether to be amused by this or offended.

Given his tone of voice, Catherine was instantly worried that he *was* taking offense and she didn't want him to. She'd meant it as a compliment.

"Not junk," she protested with feeling. "What I'm selling in the shop are rescued artifacts that once figured very prominently in people's lives."

To underscore her point, Catherine motioned toward the shelves directly behind her. Shelves she had so painstakingly arranged. The shelves were filled with newly cleaned merchandise, shown off to their best possible advantage. It was a potpourri of objects in all sorts of bright colors.

Currently, the sun was playing off the surface of several of the pieces, highlighting the metal and making them gleam like mysterious talismans.

"Everything you see here is vintage chic," she told him proudly.

He inclined his head, taking a closer look, then raised one shoulder in a half shrug. "If you say so," he murmured. Ever practical, he turned his attention to something that he was better equipped to understand. "Who are you getting to put your sign up?"

Catherine turned around to look through the window in the general direction he'd nodded in and said, "I hadn't thought about 'getting' someone. I figured that I'd just do it myself—"

That was what he was afraid of.

Cody looked at her up and down slowly, taking full measure of her. His expression when he finished clearly said that he had found her wanting.

He snorted rather than say anything outright. His point driven home, he then asked, "You got that ladder handy?" referring to the one she'd fallen off of at their first meeting.

Did he think she was a complete helpless idiot? she wondered. How else did he think she was going to get up to the roof to hang the sign?

"Yes, it's in the back." The words were hardly out of her mouth when she saw Cody start to walk to the back room. The man was just taking over, she thought. She liked him, liked his company, but that couldn't be allowed to happen.

"Where are you going?" she wanted to know.

"To get your ladder and hang that sign up for you," Cody threw over his shoulder as he disappeared into the back room.

She didn't want him to feel obligated to do anything except give her a little input on what he thought of certain things. That was their deal.

Hurrying after Cody, Catherine stopped short of the back room doorway because he was already coming out. He had the ladder mounted like a giant shield over one muscular shoulder while he carried a hammer he'd spotted and pressed into service in the other.

Pivoting a hundred and eighty degrees on her heel, Catherine followed him back through the showroom. Was he just displaying his machismo? Or was he feeling obligated for some reason?

"You don't have to do this," she protested with feeling as she continued to follow him.

He paused fleetingly to give her a quick, appraising look. Catherine could have sworn she felt a flash of heat pass through her.

That had to stop, she silently upbraided herself. She had no time to react to Cody in those terms. She had a business to launch.

"Yeah, I do," he answered with finality. "I'm better at hanging up a sign than I am at setting broken bones."

She was right behind him, step for step. "Contrary to what you might think, I'm not some helpless woman who's all thumbs," she informed him. "And I'm not a klutz. I've got great balance and I'm very handy."

"Good for you," he fired back. "Where I come from, men don't stand around watching women do this kind of work," he told her with feeling. He was thinking specifically of Caroline's husband. Rory Connors would have liked nothing better than to never have to move another muscle in his body for as long as he lived if he didn't want to.

That no-good SOB had his baby sister doing all the heavy work—and she wasn't up to half of it. He was certain that was why Caroline had lost the baby she was carrying before it had even gotten through its first trimester. He recalled with anger that his brother-in-law had expressed no remorse over the loss that had all but completely devastated Caroline.

On the contrary, Connors had actually been relieved, saying that there was no room for "brats" in his life right now.

Or ever, Cody suspected. The man was far too egotistical and self-centered to share Caroline with even a baby.

Cody slowly became aware that Catherine was laughing. When he looked at her quizzically, waiting for an explanation, the woman was quick to let him in on the joke.

"Um, this might not have occurred to you but you and I come from the exact same place," she pointed out.

He frowned as he steadied the ladder, picked up the sign and then began to climb up. She was right. "Yeah, well, then you should know that I wasn't about to have you climbing up to the top, tottering on the ladder while you tried to hang this sign up. I was quick enough to catch you last time. I might not be this time."

"I wasn't going to *try* to hang it up," she corrected with just a slight edge to her voice. She liked him and she knew he meant well, but she didn't like being thought of as inept. "I was *going* to hang it up. There's not exactly a need for an engineering degree when it comes to hanging up a sign," Catherine pointed out. "And I figure I've filled my quota of falling off ladders. That was my first time and my *only* time," she emphasized.

Cody looked down at her in silence for a long moment. For a brief second, she thought that he was just going to let go of the sign, climb down off the ladder and walk away.

But then, uttering an unintelligible noise—at least she couldn't make any sense of it—Cody turned his attention to what had brought him up here in the first place. With an amazingly accurate eye, he hung the sign exactly in the middle, directly over the doorway. He did it without bothering to measure first, without resorting to any sort of gauges and without asking her for any visual guidance from her vantage point.

The man had a fantastic eye, she thought. It was obvious that he was a natural. One of those incredibly gifted souls who could build an entire building using a bent spoon, a wad of chewing gum and a set of popsicle sticks. He was creative without even knowing that he was. She was more convinced than ever that she had chosen the right man as her inspiration. He obviously came with fringe benefits—and muscles, she noted.

Her stomach seemed to tighten of its own accord.

Catherine stepped back, admiring the sign. "That's absolutely perfect," she pronounced as he came back down the ladder.

He didn't bother looking up at his handiwork. Instead, he merely said, "I know."

That sort of statement reeked of conceit, and yet, she realized, the man wasn't conceited, nor did he actually sound that way. Instead, what he sounded was self-assured. He was a man who knew his limitations—if he actually possessed any—and he was obviously fairly comfortable in his own skin.

That, she knew, wasn't often the case. Most people were usually hounded by insecurities, whether large or small.

"Must be nice," Catherine couldn't help commenting to him.

Again Cody raised a quizzical eyebrow as he looked at her, waiting for some sort of explanation or further elaboration.

"What is?" he finally asked when she didn't elaborate further.

Her eyes met his. She consciously banked down the shiver that rose within her. "Being so confident."

"Not a matter of confidence," Cody told her. "Just a matter of knowing what I can and can't do."

She thought that was one and the same, but it was obviously different to him.

Be that as it may, she had no intention of getting into a discussion with Cody over this. She didn't want this cowboy—who really did come across like the genuine article to her—to think she was trying to challenge him or trip him up. He seemed just perfect the way he was and she was fairly certain it would help business along for her if she could tap into this man's likes and preferences. There had to be a lot more like him around here, right? And she wanted her merchandise to appeal to people with his sensibilities and preferences.

Cody took the ladder and returned it to the back room, pausing next to her just for a moment to ask, "Got anything else you need hung up?"

Catherine smiled as she shook her head. "Not at the moment," she replied.

In response, he nodded his head and continued on his way. He replaced the ladder where he had found it, along with the hammer.

"I would, however, like to get your input on a few things," she said, raising her voice so that it followed him into the back room.

He didn't answer until he came out again. "Well, I'm here, might as well use me. Ask away," he told her.

Might as well use me. Now there was a straight line if ever there was one, she couldn't help thinking as she bit her tongue to keep quiet.

Instead, she beckoned Cody over to the counter where she had her laptop up and running. She'd set it up the minute she'd come in this morning, thinking to get a little online shopping done whenever she felt like taking a break. She had all the sites bookmarked.

"I've been looking through some eBay auctions of things I thought would be perfect for the shop," she told Cody.

"So get them," he advised.

"I'd like a second opinion," she told him honestly. And that second opinion was where he came in. That was the deal.

"Why?" he wanted to know. "Don't you trust your own judgment?"

"Yes I do," she said. "But it's always good to have reinforcement."

He considered her words. The woman wasn't headstrong, but she wasn't wishy-washy, either. He found himself nodding in silent approval of this woman he'd just barely met.

Catherine Clifton was a good blend of various personalities, he thought. She was definitely different from most of the women he had interacted with since Renee's passing. It wasn't that he was in the market for another wife—one heartache in his lifetime was more than enough for him—but hell, at his age he wasn't looking to up and join a monastery, either.

Only problem was, most of the women around here fell into two groups. The first group was mainly concerned with trivial things—things like what outfit or hairstyle looked best on them. Mindless things. And then there was that other group. The women who made no secret of the fact that they felt he was "broken" and they knew just how to "fix" him.

He wasn't about to let that group get their hands on him, not by a hell of a long shot, he thought. He wasn't "broken," at least, not in a way that any of them could even begin to heal, and he wasn't lonely, either. At least, not lonely enough to take up with any of those women for more than a couple of days or so. After that, he just lost patience with them, preferring his own company or the company of his horses to being subjected to endless, mindless chatter that somehow always managed to work the phrase "How do I look?" into the conversation.

Any conversation.

Looking at Catherine now, he couldn't help wondering if ultimately she was going to fall into one of those two categories. He was probably wrong, but he had a hunch that she wasn't.

A larger part of him felt that it really didn't matter either way.

But just the smallest part of him hoped that he was right.

Chapter Four

"You planning on selling used clothes in the store, too?" Cody wanted to know when she showed him some of the things she'd acquired.

While the main focus of the shop was going to remain on vintage pieces of furniture, Catherine thought that bringing in a few items of clothing might actually draw in more potential customers and provide her clientele an eclectic selection to choose from. She intended to display the clothing in the same section of the shop that Cody had found the fringed coin purse he'd sent to his sister.

"They're not used," Catherine corrected, employing a euphemism. "They're pre-owned."

Cody snorted. "Fancy words," he said, dismissing the term she'd substituted with a wave of his hand. Whatever she called them, if someone had worn them before, the clothes were still used.

To his surprise, Catherine didn't argue. "Yes, they are, and they're meant to convey a different image," she told him. To show him what she meant, she opened up a large cardboard box. Inside were the various articles of clothing that she had managed to collect so far. "Everything in here has been cleaned, pressed and, in some cases, mended," she allowed. "But they're not rags," she quickly specified, guessing what was going through Cody's mind. She raised her eyes to his face. "Every item in here has a story. Every castoff has potential."

Cody realized that she was looking at him and not at anything in particular that she had inside the box. For a second, he was going to ask her if she was trying to tell him something, then decided he was probably reading far too much into her tone.

Glancing at the contents of the box, he saw a brightly beaded shirt and a multicolored scarf that would have looked more at home around her neck lying right on top of the pile of clothing.

He fingered the scarf for a second. *Soft,* he thought. Just like her skin.

Now how the hell would he have known that? A little unnerved, he let the scarf drop back into the box.

"So this is going to be like a thrift shop?" he asked, trying to get a handle on what her actual intent was.

A thrift shop tended to suggest rock-bottom prices, and she was going for an image that was a little more exclusive than that.

"No, it's not going to be *that* inexpensive," she explained with a smile. "I'm thinking more along the lines that one man's 'junk' can turn out to be another man's treasure."

Cody rummaged a little deeper into the box, then

laughed shortly. There was nothing exactly impressive to be found in there.

A hint of amusement was evident in his eyes when he looked at her. "Kind of stretching the word 'treasure' a mite, aren't you?"

She didn't quite see it that way. "It's like that saying about beauty being in the eyes of the beholder," Catherine pointed out. "You never know what might appeal to a person." And then she smiled broadly at him. "Which is what I have you for."

Cody looked at the woman he'd struck a bargain with. Maybe he needed to rethink this arrangement a bit. Since she *had* given him that purse for Caroline in exchange for his so-called services, he felt obligated to give her *something* in return. But at the moment, that wasn't as easy as it might have sounded to an outsider. The truth of it was, he really had very few "likes" himself. For him it had always been more of a case of just "making do."

Cody felt it was only right to try to explain that to her. "I'm a simple man, Catherine," he told her. "If you're waiting for me to get excited about something, you've got a long wait ahead of you."

There was that shiver again, Catherine thought as it shimmied up and down her spine. That wonderful/ strange sensation that insisted on undulating along her back as if she was anticipating something.

Something from him.

Pressing her lips together, Catherine did her best to block the feeling. To ignore it and just focus on the business at hand.

Still, she couldn't help saying, "I'm sure it'll be worth waiting for when it finally happens."

Damn, but there was something about this woman, Cody caught himself thinking, the thought flashing across his mind completely out of the blue. Something that stirred up his insides like one of those food processors he'd seen demonstrated once. All without any warning.

And when she tilted her head just like that—as if that could help her understand something—the sun wound up getting caught in her hair and he could see reddish streaks lacing through it.

Warming his blood.

Warming him.

And, yeah, by God, tempting him, he silently admitted.

Maybe he should just kiss her and get it over with, Cody thought, doing his best to be pragmatic. That way, maybe his thoughts would finally stop going where they didn't belong and he could get back to focusing on "paying up his debt" to her. He didn't like being beholden to anyone, even someone as pretty as Catherine.

For just the tiniest split second, he debated acting on the thought. Debated kissing her purely for practical reasons.

He even leaned into her a little. And once he did, he started to go through the rest of the motions. His eyes held her prisoner just as much as hers managed to hold him in the same cell.

His lips were almost touching hers—

And then the bell over the doorway went off, splintering the moment. Breaking the mood.

Announcing the presence of another person entering their private space.

Acute discomfort, laced through with a prickly dose

of guilt, had Cody taking a step back away from his intended target before he looked in the direction of the offending doorway.

"I thought you said you were closed," he said to Catherine, his tone dark.

It almost sounded like an accusation, Catherine thought, even as she tried to figure out exactly what had just happened here—and what hadn't happened.

"I am," she finally answered, the words emerging from her lips in slow, confused motion.

"But she's not closed to family," the person walking into the shop cheerfully declared. The smile in the young woman's voice was only rivaled by the one on her face. "Are you, Cate?"

A wave of disappointment washed over Catherine, although she wasn't altogether certain why or what it was that she was disappointed about. It took her a moment to catch her breath.

Belatedly, she looked toward the source of the cheery voice and identified the young woman for Cody. "C.C."

"Well, at least you still recognize me." Her youngest sister laughed. "That's hopeful." She looked pleased with the observation. Stepping forward as she took the muffler off from around her neck, C.C. put her hand out to her sister's friend. "Hi, I'm the cheerful sister." She cocked her head the exact same way that Catherine did. "And you are?" She waited for the man to identify himself.

"Just leaving," Cody replied gruffly, a feeling of uncustomary awkwardness invading him. It was a strange feeling and he couldn't say that he much cared for it.

"Well, Mister 'Just Leaving,'" C.C. said, tongue in cheek as she made her request, "please don't do it on my account. I just dropped by to see how things were going and to ask my big sister if she needed a hand for a few hours." Her grin grew to almost huge proportions as her eyes swept over the man she'd seen standing almost intimately close to her sister. "You obviously don't," she concluded, turning toward Catherine. There was blanket approval in C.C.'s eyes—as well as admiration and perhaps just the tiniest touch of envy. "You seem to be doing just fine." Her eyes all but danced as she turned toward the door again. "I'll just leave you two alone and—"

"No, stay," Cody said. It was very close to sounding like an order. "I was just going."

The grin—or was that a smirk, Cody wondered—remained as Catherine's younger sister seemed to take careful measure of him.

"You didn't look as if you were just going when I came in," she told him. "From where I was standing, you looked like you'd just arrived."

If that was a riddle, he had no time to untangle it. He missed the very annoyed look that Catherine shot at her sister. Glancing at C.C., he mumbled something that sounded like "nice meeting you" without any conviction whatsoever and then addressed Catherine. "I'll be seeing you," he told her with a nod of his head.

A few strides toward the door and then he was gone.

"I sure hope so," C.C. murmured under her breath as the door closed again. The tiny bell needlessly announced his departure. Turning on her heel to look at her sister, C.C. declared with no small enthusiasm, "If you're stocking those in the store, I'll take twelve."

"C.C.—" There was a warning note in Catherine's voice.

"Okay, okay," C.C. relented. "I'm being greedy. I'll take ten." Seeing her older sister's frown deepen, she stopped teasing. Kind of. "Who *was* that masked man?" she wanted to know. "He was absolutely, blood-pumpingly gorgeous."

There was no point in telling C.C. that what she'd just said made no sense. There were times when her youngest sister lived on a planet all her own.

So instead, Catherine simply said, "That was Cody Overton."

There was a great deal more to this man than just a name, C.C. thought. Her sister might not be aware of the sparks of electricity she'd just seen flying between them, but she definitely was. It's a wonder neither one of them had any of their skin singed.

"And?" C.C. wanted to know.

Catherine looked at the younger girl, completely confused. "And what?"

C.C. looked at her closely, as if she was attempting to delve into her sister's mind. With absolutely no luck at the moment. So she asked, "And have you been holding out on us?"

"Holding out?" Catherine repeated, at this point very thoroughly confused. There was no "holding out." Her life and what she did was an open book. A *boring* one, granted, but an open one nonetheless. She had no idea what C.C. was talking about.

C.C. gravitated toward the box of clothes that Catherine had just opened. Her attention was instantly captivated by the top two items, each of which she took out and held up for closer examination. She definitely liked what she saw.

"You know, like a secret lover," C.C. elaborated absently. Holding the beaded shirt against herself, C.C. smoothed it down into place. She tried to imagine what it would look like coupled with her favorite pair of jeans. It would definitely turn heads, she concluded. Holding the shirt up, she asked Catherine, "Hey, you give discounts to relatives?"

Pressing the blouse against her upper torso, C.C. went in search of a mirror or some sort of shiny surface to give her an idea what she looked like in the shirt.

"Only if I don't disown them," Catherine fired back. And then she softened just a little. "Seriously, what are you doing here?"

"'Seriously,' I came to help out for a few hours," C.C. told her again. And then a touch of remorse entered her voice. "I didn't mean to break something up."

"You didn't," Catherine quickly assured her.

C.C. laughed, shaking her head. Was her sister in denial—or just trying to pretend nothing was going on for her benefit?

"You obviously weren't paying attention," she chided, then tossed in an accusation for good measure. "You've been holding out on me." Rather than be annoyed, C.C. was delighted with this turn of events. "Have you known him long?"

Catherine was completely speechless at the way her youngest sister could jump to conclusions without any sort of real input at all. She made it sound as if there was something going on—and there wasn't.

"A couple of hours," she finally told her sister, hoping that was the end of it.

But this was C.C. and the "end" was a long way away, Catherine thought with a mental groan.

"Looked like he knew you a lot better than that,"

C.C. commented, putting the shirt on the counter before going on to explore the rest of the box's contents.

Catherine deliberately took the faded, flared jeans out of C.C.'s hands. She didn't want her sister "buying" the entire contents of the box. Knowing C.C., what she'd get was a series of IOUs that C.C. would conveniently forget about and that she herself would have no intentions of collecting on. Family was family through thick and thin and sales receipts.

"How is it you don't get a nose bleed from jumping to conclusions like that?" Catherine asked her matter-of-factly.

Rather than answer, C.C. cocked her head as she eyed Catherine again. She had no intentions of having her sister distract her. Something was up—and she had a pretty good idea what that something was all about.

"Methinks the lady doth protest too much," C.C. declared in a pseudo-cultured voice.

"What the 'lady' is desperately trying to do is keep from strangling her youngest sister to death," Catherine countered between clenched teeth.

She loved everyone in her family more than words could possibly begin to describe, but there were times when they—collectively and individually—got to be just too much for her. That was when she'd engineer a mini-getaway—sometimes all she needed was a few hours alone. But this time, she had a feeling she might need just to "disappear" for more than an hour—or five.

Despite the threat—obviously an empty one, C.C. thought—she didn't back off. For one, she was having far too good a time with this. For another, she knew that Catherine didn't even yell, so murder seemed as if it would be a little out of her comfort zone.

"Am I getting too close?" C.C. asked her.

"To your own demise?" Catherine shot back, then added a confirmation. "Yes."

For a second, C.C. did back off, but only to study her subject. "You know, I don't think I've ever seen you like this before." For C.C. there was only one conclusion to be drawn. "You must really like this guy."

Catherine's slender shoulders rose and then fell again in a dismissive shrug. "He's just a cowboy—"

"Yeah, I know." C.C.'s voice was almost dreamy as she talked. "I really thought he'd mount his horse and go riding off into the sunset. *Where* have you been keeping him all this time?" she wanted to know, refusing to believe that Catherine had just stumbled across this man a matter of hours ago, the way she'd alluded.

Catherine sighed. Her sister was a hopeless romantic and ever since Calista had announced plans for her upcoming wedding, C.C. had gone off on some impossible tangent, seeing potential grooms behind every tree and rock. She was surprised that the girl hadn't eloped with someone by now.

Surprised and grateful, Catherine added silently before tackling C.C.'s overly fertile imagination one last time.

"Once and for all, C.C., I haven't been 'keeping' Cody anywhere. He walked in here three days ago, looking to buy a birthday present for his sister. When he spotted a fringed coin purse, I decided to make him a trade—I'd let him have the coin purse for free in exchange for his opinion on a few items I was going to be carrying in the shop." She could see by the expression on her sister's face that C.C. just wasn't buying into this. Damn, but that girl could be stubborn. "I thought

I'd try to appeal to his demographic," Catherine tacked on, feeling almost helpless.

"So what you're saying is that you're planning on only selling to hopelessly sexy cowboys with killer eyes?" There were dimples winking in and out of the corners of her mouth as she made no effort to keep the amused grin off her lips.

For now Catherine threw in the towel. "Why don't you see if Calista needs help with her wedding plans?" she suggested forcefully.

"I'd rather stay here and torture you," C.C. told her with a straight face. But when she saw the exasperated look that entered Catherine's chocolate eyes, she held up her hands in protest. "Okay, okay, I'll cease and desist, I promise." And then a serious look flitted across her face as she said, "But I am sorry."

Okay, what was *this* about? "About what?" she asked aloud.

Wasn't Catherine paying *any* attention? "That I walked in at the wrong time. From where I was standing, it looked as if your so-called 'Mr. Demographic' was just about to kiss you—and would have if I hadn't picked just then to come barging in."

If she were being honest, Catherine would have had to admit that she'd been pretty certain that he *was* going to kiss her just then. But then, maybe this had all worked out for the best anyway.

"That's just your imagination," Catherine insisted, wanting the book to be closed.

Rather than continue the argument, C.C. merely shrugged. "Okay, if you say so, Cate. But I *was* serious when I said that I came here to help you out in the store for a little bit. I don't have to be anywhere for a few hours and I thought you might want some help sorting all this stuff. Unless, of course, you want to save it for Mr. Strong, Silent Type," C.C. amended.

Instead of answering, Catherine went into the back room. When she emerged again, she was armed with a large feather duster. The moment she was close to C.C., she placed the feather duster into her sister's hand.

"Here, if you really want to be useful, start dusting from the back to the front," she instructed. "I don't think this place has had a once-over since before Jasper Fowler got arrested."

"That's an awful lot of dust," C.C. commented.

"I know," Catherine agreed sympathetically. "So I guess you'd better get started if you want to finish before next Easter."

C.C. saluted her with the feather duster. "Your word is my command, Cate." She grinned as she looked around. "This really is pretty exciting," she agreed. "When are you opening for business again?" she asked as she started dusting.

Catherine thought of her target date. It was breathing down her neck. How did it get to be so late in the month? "Too soon," she murmured.

"Well, if you don't think you'll be ready in time, you could always ask Mr. Delicious Cowboy to come riding to your rescue."

"Just dust," Catherine ordered, pointing to an area that was completely obscured by dust.

Her sister laughed and saluted with the hilt of the duster. "Yes'm."

Catherine nodded her head and smiled at C.C.'s "obedient" response. She had to admit, she liked the sound of that. Especially after all these years.

"You're finally catching on, C.C.," she told her sister.

"I could say the same thing about you," she heard C.C. murmur under her breath.

About to make another comment, Catherine decided to hold her piece instead. A great deal more would get done in the store in the long run if she just pretended not to have heard C.C.'s last reply.

Chapter Five

That had been a very close call, Cody told himself as he drove his truck over to the General Store. He'd nearly forgotten to pick up the things that had supposedly brought him into Thunder Canyon in the first place. He could just picture what Hank and Kurt would say about that.

The ranch hands wouldn't say anything to him directly, but there'd be winks and nods and knowing nudges. He could damn well do without that.

But that wasn't what he actually regarded as his "close call."

If that blonde girl hadn't come into Catherine's store just when she did, he probably would have wound up kissing Catherine.

Not a good idea.

Not that he hadn't kissed anyone in the last eight years. He had. He'd done a lot more than just kissed those other women, too, but he had an uneasy feeling that while the other women he'd been with were just a way for him to satisfy the physical need he occasionally experienced, kissing the enthusiastic store owner would lead him down a whole different path.

Not one he was planning to take. Ever.

Anyone could see that Catherine Clifton wasn't like the others.

There was a purpose to her, one that did *not* include fixing or changing him. She was the first woman he'd come across in a long time who didn't strike him as being just one-dimensional. There was substance to her. He found he could carry on a conversation with her without having his mind drift off somewhere in the middle because he was bored.

No, Cody thought as he absently made his way through the General Store's aisles, looking for the items he'd said he was bringing back, the woman definitely wasn't boring.

Far from it.

He was attracted to her and therein lay his problem. He didn't want to be attracted to her, didn't want to be attracted to anyone. A strong enough attraction could lead to caring and that could lead to disaster. He knew that firsthand.

Caring was asking to have his heart ripped out of his chest and barbecued on a bed of hot coals when he least expected it.

Loving someone left you vulnerable to all sorts of things.

Been there, done that, Cody thought with finality, deliberately shutting the door on the very idea that he could *ever* allow himself to go down that particular path again.

The thought abruptly had him coming to a mental skidding halt.

What the hell was going on here? How had he gone from *almost* kissing Catherine to having his heart extracted without benefit of an anesthetic?

That whole analogy was way too dramatic for him.

Rolling it over in his head now, it seemed more like something one of the women he'd gone out with after Renee's passing might have said.

He wasn't being himself.

Maybe he *should* have kissed her, Cody decided, rethinking the situation. Just to show himself that he could take it or leave it—and her—whenever he felt like it.

Just to prove to himself that the feisty shop owner had no power over him.

"Will there be anything else, Cody?" the older man behind the checkout counter asked him politely. All his groceries were tabulated and neatly stacked to the side, waiting to be packed up.

Cody blinked, coming out of his self-imposed mental fog as he suddenly realized that he'd come to a dead stop at the checkout counter and hadn't moved, even after he'd paid his bill.

The man he'd handed the cash to had to think that he was a little bit crazy just to remain standing there as if he was trying to imitate a statue.

"No, thanks." He forced what passed for a smile to his lips for the clerk's benefit. "That's everything," he said to him.

The man looked at him thoughtfully and with just

the smallest measure of concern. "Everything all right, Cody?" he inquired.

"Everything's fine, Jake," Cody replied immediately. His tone left no opening for any sort of further exchange. He wasn't one to discuss *anything* that was going on in his private life.

Taking the grocery bags off the counter, he hefted them outside to his truck and secured them in the back.

Without a backward glance—at the store clerk or at Real Vintage Cowboy—the shop was located down the street—Cody climbed into the cab of his truck, pointed it in the direction of his ranch and drove off.

Driving past Catherine's shop, there was a part of him that actually toyed with the idea of walking right back in and getting that damn kiss out of the way.

Another part of him—the part that wound up winning—thought it might be a better idea if he slept on his impulse first.

Then, if he still felt that he needed to get this whole thing out in the open and out of his system, he could always come back another day and do whatever he felt he had to do.

But right now, he decided, it was better for all concerned if he just kept driving and ignored any and all impulses—sharp or otherwise—that telegraphed themselves through him.

Cody frowned.

Deeply.

He'd never cared for complications, and this definitely felt like one hell of a complication in the making.

With effort, he forced his thoughts to focus on what needed to be attended to next on the ranch. After all, his ranch was the really important thing.

He had horses to train and ranch hands to pay, Cody reminded himself. Beyond that, nothing else mattered.

Or, at least, it wasn't supposed to.

It was just by accident that Cody was in the house two mornings later to hear the phone ring. Most days, he'd already be out, either helping to clean the stables or in the corral, working with and training the quarter horses.

For the most part, he looked upon a phone as strictly a convenience for him in case he had to call a vet for one of his horses. Otherwise, he looked upon it as just another decoration hanging next to the calendar on the kitchen wall.

He didn't really like being on the receiving end of a phone call.

There was a reason for that.

The ringing phone brought back bad memories. It reminded him of the time someone from the hospital had called to tell him that there'd been an accident and that his parents wouldn't be coming home.

Ever.

He'd been eighteen at the time, an adult by legal standards. But it had hit him hard, right in his gut, stripping him of his years and making him feel like some helpless kid again.

Suddenly, just like that, he found himself orphaned. Orphaned and yet catapulted into the scary position of being head of the household. And if that hadn't been intimidating enough, he also became—just like that—Caroline's legal guardian since his sister was four years younger than he was and, at the time, still a minor.

Cody had always been his own person, but suddenly,

without warning, he'd been thrown headlong into the deep end of the pool. It was up to him to make all the decisions. Decisions about his parents' funeral arrangements, about whether to sell the ranch or try to make a go of it. Most frightening of all, he had to make decisions involving his sister's welfare. Quick decisions. If he hadn't been willing to become her legal guardian, Caroline would have become a ward of the court for the next four years of her life.

As far as he was concerned, that part really required no debating at all. There was no way on earth that he would have allowed his sister to be swallowed up by the system.

One isolated early morning phone call and his entire life had changed. Cody had aged at least ten years in the small space of time between when he picked up the receiver and when he hung it up again.

Maybe Caroline would have been better off if he *had* agreed to let the court take her and place her in a foster home, he thought now. At least then she wouldn't have met that loser of a husband of hers and Rory wouldn't be controlling her the way he did.

All this shot through Cody's mind as he stared at the ringing phone on his kitchen wall. He debated just letting the phone go on ringing until whoever was on the other end hung up, but ultimately that was the coward's way out. He'd never been a coward.

With a sigh, Cody picked up the receiver and said, "Hello?"

"Cody?"

The high, female voice on the other end was timid. Despite the fact that he was hardly ever on the phone and that he hadn't heard from her in more than a year, he recognized the voice immediately.

"Hi, Caroline." He glanced at the calendar next to the phone to verify the date before saying, "Happy Birthday."

"Thank you," she responded warmly. "Your present came in the mail yesterday. I just called to tell you that I really love it."

"You weren't supposed to open it until today," he told her.

Caroline laughed softly and just for a moment, she sounded the way she used to, before reality had sliced through her life.

"I couldn't wait."

"Well, that hasn't changed any," Cody noted.

He recalled that when Caroline had been a little girl, his sister couldn't wait to open her gifts. No matter how meager they might have been, she was always excited, always appreciative, acting as if she'd received spectacular treasures instead of the mundane, practical gifts that she found under the tree each year, Cody remembered.

"I'm sure you have better use for your money than to spend it on me," Caroline was saying. "A card would have been more than enough." She paused for a moment, then added in a soft, almost shy whisper, "Thank you for remembering."

Cody didn't know how to respond to that. Moreover, he couldn't shake the feeling that something was off, was wrong. He knew he couldn't pry. That would only lead to an exchange of words that would make him lose his temper, and he didn't want to get into an argument with his sister today, not on her birthday.

His sister was a lot more loyal than that scum, otherwise known as her husband, deserved, Cody thought darkly.

He really wished there was a way to convince her to leave the no-account, wasted piece of flesh. But there wasn't.

"Why shouldn't I remember?" he finally asked. "You're my sister and it's not like I've twelve others to keep track of."

He'd often thought, because there was just the two of them after their parents were killed, that when he'd gotten married, Caroline had followed suit not long afterward because she was very vulnerable and Rory had used that to his advantage. He was attentive and sweet to her just long enough to get her to marry him.

He felt responsible for his sister's unhappiness even though both he and Renee had invited Caroline to come live with them. Caroline had turned them down, saying that newlyweds needed to be alone.

Only the look in her eyes had told him how truly lonely his sister actually felt. He shouldn't have listened to her. He should have *insisted* that she come live with them. But he'd been selfish. He'd wanted to be alone with Renee.

And Caroline was the one who wound up paying the price for that.

Rory had taken advantage of her loneliness. That alone would earn the man his place in hell. And the sooner the better.

"It was very sweet of you," Caroline told him. He could have sworn Caroline sounded as if she was about to say something more, but then her tone suddenly changed. A nervous uneasiness all but vibrated in her throat. "I've got to go. Thank you," she said again, the words rushing out of her mouth.

The hell with tiptoeing around because it was her birthday. Something was definitely not right here.

"Caroline, what's wrong?" he asked. But there was no answer. He strained to hear something, a telltale sound. But there was nothing. "Caroline?" Cody called, more loudly this time.

His sister had hung up. But just before the connection had gone dead, Cody could have sworn he had heard a male voice yelling Caroline's name in the background.

Cody scowled.

Caroline jumped every time her husband so much as snapped his fingers. Was she just being skittish or was there more behind her behavior than that?

Did that loser abuse her?

Cody clenched his fists at his sides in frustrated, impotent anger. There wasn't anything he could do. Caroline wouldn't listen to reason. Wouldn't listen to him when he'd all but begged her to leave that miserable excuse for a human being.

The last time he had gotten between Caroline and her husband, Rory had taken her and moved to another state. Cody had an uneasy feeling that if he turned up on his sister's doorstep, this time Rory would make sure that they completely disappeared without leaving so much as a forwarding address. Rory wouldn't put up with any interference. The man acted like a malevolent dictator who was exceedingly possessive of his tiny kingdom. Everything had to go through him.

Trying to convince Caroline to leave her husband wasn't going to work. She had to come to that conclusion on her own for it to actually take root and happen. He was powerless to do anything except pray that somebody would mistake Rory for a bear and shoot him.

He would have gladly volunteered to be the one.

But knowing he was powerless to do anything and living with it were two very different things. There were times when he was convinced that he could easily kill Rory with his bare hands. The man brought out the very worst in him.

Restless, Cody found himself pacing around the kitchen after he'd hung up. As the feeling kept building rather than dissipating, Cody decided that maybe a trip into town might help calm him down.

For some strange reason, Catherine and that ridiculously named shop of hers—what the hell was a Real Vintage Cowboy, anyway?—had a calming, almost peaceful effect on him.

When she wasn't stirring him up, he added with a bemused smile on his face.

Making his decision, Cody took his car keys off the peg where he kept them when he was home and went to get his truck.

The smile Catherine flashed at him when he walked into her showroom an hour later told him that he'd made the right decision.

The fact that it ignited a fire in his gut was beside the point.

What he needed right now was a little distraction. Fortunately, that was *exactly* what happened each time he came into the store. He got distracted.

And maybe a little lost in those chocolate eyes of hers, he added silently.

"I was hoping you'd come in today," Catherine told him, quickly crossing over to Cody.

She didn't strike him as someone who just stood around, wishing for something to happen. The woman was a doer.

"Why didn't you call me?" he wanted to know. After all, it wasn't as if he hadn't given her his number.

The answer Caroline gave surprised him. "Because I didn't feel I had the right to disturb you if you were busy working. After all, your ranch does have to come first."

A person who didn't think that the world revolved exclusively around them, he thought. If someone would have asked him, he would have said that he thought that was an attribute that only his late wife and his sister possessed. For the most part, he found people to be more and more self-centered.

He looked at Catherine for a long moment, debating whether or not to tell her that he came into town because he wanted to see her.

His underlying need for caution had him saying instead, "I needed a break for a while."

She nodded, not questioning his reasons for coming, just happy that he had.

"I'll try not to overwork you," she promised with a wink, then grew serious. "But I did want to ask your opinion on a few things that I found online." Tugging a little on his arm, she drew him over to the counter where she had set up her laptop. Turning the laptop so that it faced him, she said, "Take a look at this."

But rather than looking at the screen, Cody glanced around the shop first.

She'd done a lot of work on it since he'd been here two days ago. Didn't the woman ever sleep? Or did she have a legion of helpers when he wasn't around?

"How do you manage to do it all?" he wanted to know, allowing a note of admiration to slip through.

Catherine wasn't sure she was following him. "Excuse me?"

"The shop's a lot cleaner and neater than the last time I saw it," he elaborated. "And you've obviously had time to go looking on the internet—"

There were a lot more items in the shop now than there had been the last time he'd been here. Unless she had a warehouse somewhere close by, this had all been bought and shipped in the last couple of days.

Looking on the internet. Catherine smiled at his terminology. "It's called browsing," she supplied helpfully.

"It's called being superhuman," he countered. Just cleaning the place up like this would have required a great deal of her time. Yet she didn't look wilted. "Do you sleep at all?"

Catherine laughed. "Every day and a half I hang upside down in the closet for a quick nap."

He looked at her for a long, long moment, then declared, "You are one very strange lady, Catherine Clifton. You know that?"

Her grin widened. "I just know what I want, that's all," she replied, then tugged on his arm again, this time a little more insistently. "Now come and look at these things and tell me what you think."

What I think is that I have a tiger by the tail, he said silently.

"Might as well," he said out loud, sounding not nearly as reluctant as he might have just a few days ago. "Since I'm here," he tacked on.

"Since you're here," Catherine echoed warmly, her eyes crinkling as her smile deepened.

He did his best not to notice, but his best wasn't quite good enough.

The warmth she generated inside of him could have toasted marshmallows if the need arose.

Chapter Six

Cody sighed.

He and Catherine had been going over various estate sale sites on her laptop for a while now and next to nothing had stirred his interest. Certainly nothing he would have gone out of his way to own.

While he did like having an excuse to be around this vibrant woman whose very presence sucked the solemnity out of his existence, he had to be honest with her. She was wasting her time having him do this.

"You know," he began, turning away from the laptop. "I really think you should get someone else to help you with this."

Catherine raised her eyes from the laptop screen and looked at him for a long moment. She tried to gauge what his thoughts were, but she could have saved herself the trouble. The man had an expression that totally defied penetration.

Having nothing to lose, she took a stab at his reasons for saying what he just had. "You don't want to do this anymore?"

"It's not a matter of not wanting to do it," he corrected. Because, if he were being honest with her, he rather enjoyed these little impromptu sessions. He wouldn't have come into town so often in the last week if he didn't. He liked her company and, despite their different way of viewing things, they were comfortable with one another.

But that wasn't the point behind all this, was it?

"Then what?" she prodded.

She wasn't accustomed to dealing with someone who had to have words coaxed out of him. In her family, silence was something that only occurred if everyone happened to be asleep at the same time.

Otherwise, the air was filled with the hum of voices constantly crisscrossing one another. Sometimes several at the same time.

Her father had once referred to the boisterous exchange of words and opinions as a cacophony. She thought that was really an excellent word for it. There certainly was no denying that they were a noisy bunch of people.

Cody was the exact opposite. He had made silence into an art form. The man kept his peace inordinately long, sometimes not even speaking when he was spoken to. He didn't even make any noise when he entered a room. If she hadn't had a bell mounted against the front door, she would have never even heard him walking into the shop that first day.

"I just don't think I'm doing you any good," Cody confessed. She was trying to attract business and appeal to a certain age and income bracket. But while he fit the two requirements, he just was *not* into the kind of things that everyone else was. "I'm not your average guy," he pointed out.

Amen to that, Catherine thought, suppressing the smile that rose to her lips.

"So if you're trying to find things that appeal to most people," he concluded, "I'm not your man."

Ah, if only—

The thought caught her up short, coming out of the blue and utterly surprising her. It caused her to take a second—or was that a tenth?—look at this weather-worn cowboy who'd accidentally strolled into her shop.

There was no getting away from the fact that there was a certain undercurrent between them, a chemistry that she'd felt from the first moment she saw Cody and they began talking.

Or rather, *she* began talking. For the most part, Cody was just the recipient of her words, she silently amended, amused.

"When I bought the shop, I also wound up buying all the pieces that were still in it," she told him, gesturing in a vague pattern around the area. "The antiques that Fowler hadn't sold and probably had no intentions of selling."

Calista, who'd worked there part-time while waiting for her position at the mayor's office to go full-time, had told her as much. At the time, her sister had expressed confusion as to why the man would go to the trouble of owning and operating the store without any real interest in making a profit from the place.

That was before they found out that his focus had been elsewhere all along.

"So it's not like I have nothing to sell once I officially reopen the shop's doors," she concluded. There was no point in getting rid of the inventory. She'd do better just holding on to it until she could find interested buyers and collectors. Time and patience were on her side. She wasn't in this to score a fast profit. She was in for the long haul.

The long haul. That had a rather nice ring to it, she mused.

"Okay, then I don't understand," Cody confessed, confused. "If you're planning on keeping this stuff and trying to sell it, just what exactly is it you want me for?"

Catherine pressed her lips together, struggling to keep both her grin and the accompanying words that his question generated under wraps. There was a raw magnetism about the man that appealed to her on a whole different plane than any she'd ever encountered.

But Cody wasn't the type of man you said things like that to. She instinctively knew that he liked things simple. Even if they weren't.

Pausing to take a breath first, she made her case as best she could.

"I thought you could give me a more unique perspective and help me pick out things that the average person might have overlooked."

Cody chewed on that for a second, thinking it over. And then he shook his head as he hooked his thumbs through the belt loops of his jeans. "Still think you've got the wrong person."

She didn't feel that way.

"Do you care about other people's opinions about you?" she asked point-blank. When he didn't answer her immediately, she assured him, "This isn't a trick question. I'm not trying to trap you. Matter of fact, I'm trying to free you."

"No, I don't care what other people think of me," he responded.

And as for setting him free, it was going to take more than just a few innocent, glib words to do that, Cody couldn't help thinking. His soul had been entangled and trapped, basically hidden from the light of day, for the last eight years. Ever since Renee had died, leaving him alone on this isolated piece of rock, leaving him to deal with the emptiness as best as he could.

The man who didn't care what other people thought of him, *that* was the man she wanted on her team.

"I want the 'inner you' to respond to the merchandise I point out," she explained to Cody.

"And if I don't 'respond' to what you point out?" he wanted to know.

She shrugged. "Then I don't buy it. It's not like I don't have anything to sell," she reminded him with a laugh.

These last few days she'd worked hard to make the furnishings she'd found presentable. She'd painstakingly rearranged everything to show them off to their best advantage.

It still wasn't clear to Cody. Exactly what was his function at the shop? "Maybe I'm being thick here, but I don't get what you want with me if you're planning on trying to sell all this other stuff."

"Those are antiques that might appeal to the average person who fancies himself or herself to be a collector. But I'm also looking for a few unique things that would appeal to the discerning buyer."

And *those* people usually had more disposable cash

to spend than the average person, Catherine added silently. She wasn't about to say it out loud because she knew that Cody didn't quite fall into that category.

Cody looked at her uncertainly now. "And you think that I'd know what they'd want…"

His voice trailed off as he tried to make sense of what she'd just said. He really did want to follow her. Moreover, he didn't want to think of her as being like those empty-headed women who were only defined by what their husbands did. He knew in his gut that she wasn't like that.

"I think you'd know what *you* want," Catherine told him with emphasis.

"And that makes me your unique, discerning buyer?" he questioned.

The very corners of her mouth seemed to reach up to her eyes as she smiled. "Yes."

The idea of his being "unique" had Cody shaking his head in disbelief. That was the last word he would have *ever* applied to himself.

"Like I said, Catherine Clifton, you are a strange, strange lady."

"No, I'm a good businesswoman. I just want to make sure I have a good variety available for the customers. Fowler just had dusty pieces he didn't bother taking care of. The store was his 'cover,' but it's going to be *my* business."

"And you really think that you can make a go of it?" Cody wanted to know, watching her face as she answered.

Rather than give him a confident "Yes," Catherine addressed his question honestly. "I don't know, but I sure as hell am going to try."

He liked that.

Cody found himself admiring her. Catherine Clifton had drive. And that word his father liked to use when describing his mother. His father would say that she had "spunk." At the time, the word hadn't meant anything to him one way or another, but Cody understood now exactly what his father had meant and understood, too, the appeal behind it.

Taking a deep breath, Cody decided that he was ready for another round of online browsing. He nodded toward the laptop.

"Why don't you show me some more of the things you're considering buying," he suggested.

Rather than leave the laptop on the counter where it was, Catherine decided to move it over to a quaint table for two she'd acquired on her own. When she'd bought it, she'd thought that the table looked as if it would have been more at home in an old-fashioned ice cream parlor. She'd found it all but buried beneath a stack of papers and tarp at an estate sale she'd attended.

After cleaning and restoring the set, she'd brought the table and its matching two chairs into the show-room. She intended to use it as one of the themes within the shop.

"Let's get back to it, then," Catherine said with enthusiasm. She gestured for him to sit in the chair opposite hers.

"You're the boss," he allowed.

As if anyone could ever *be Cody Overton's boss,* Catherine thought, amused. She knew better.

The late afternoon sun had slanted its rays across the shop's polished wooden floor, then withdrawn again, tiptoeing away as nightfall began to slip in.

Catherine leaned back in her chair, slowly straightening her spine. It ached a little in protest. They'd been at this for several hours now without a break, she realized.

All in all, it had been a pretty productive afternoon. Out of the scores of things she'd wound up showing him, Cody had actually selected a few. She considered the session a huge success.

"I guess that's enough for one day," she told him, stretching and rotating her shoulders. Trying to undo the kinks.

She seemed completely unaware of the fact that she was thrusting her chest out, closer to him, as she stretched. Cody tried not to notice, but it was impossible not to.

He couldn't make himself look anywhere else.

The room felt decidedly warmer to him than it had just a few minutes ago.

Taking his cue from her that it was time to leave, Cody rose to his feet and picked up his hat from the counter where he'd left it.

"I guess that I'll be heading out then." But even as he said it—even though he'd been there for the better part of the day—he found himself reluctant to just walk away and leave her.

Just then, the little carved bird within the old-fashioned cuckoo clock on the wall began to announce the hour as only a cuckoo clock could.

How did it get to be so late? Catherine couldn't help wondering. It felt as if she'd just sat down and, somehow, five hours had managed to pass by.

She felt a pinch in her stomach.

They hadn't eaten anything in *hours,* she thought. It

was a short leap from her realization to an idea. "Tell you what, why don't I buy you dinner?" she suggested impulsively.

Being impulsive was new to her and she rather liked it. She'd always been the steady, reliable one. The rock her parents and everyone else relied on. She liked the new her.

She noticed the slight frown that creased Cody's mouth. "What?"

He didn't want to say anything—but it wasn't something that he felt comfortable with, so maybe saying something was for the best.

"The way I was raised," he began slowly, "a man usually asks a woman out for the first date, not the other way around."

Catherine's eyes widened. Was that what he thought this was? A date?

Well, is it? she asked herself. She decided it was safest to think of this as a nondate date.

Besides, labels were restricting and she wanted to keep what they had between them comfortable and easy. She definitely didn't want to do something that he felt was treading on his toes.

"This isn't a date," she told him. "It's just my way of saying 'thank you' for your effort. Call it professional courtesy," she suggested.

That made it sound too stiff, too mundane. *You're a man who doesn't know what he wants,* Cody's mind taunted. "So it's *not* a date." Cody eyed her as he got his facts straight.

If that's what made him happy, so be it, she told herself. "Not a date," she assured him.

"My mistake," Cody murmured, clearly embarrassed. "Sorry."

Now she was the one who was slightly confused. "There's nothing to be sorry about."

"I feel stupid," he admitted in a singular moment of honesty.

"No reason for that, either," she assured him quickly and with feeling. The dimples, like C.C.'s, in the corner of her mouth winked in and out. The man was adorable. "To be honest, I'm flattered. I didn't think you thought of me that way—as a potential date," she tacked on by way of an explanation.

The awkward moment only grew more so. Just what did she think of him?

"I'm thirty-five, I'm not dead," Cody pointed out, then thought that maybe he would have been better off if he'd just let the matter drop without being defensive about things. After all, he really didn't want her to think he was trying to get something going between them.

Although, he had to admit, whatever there was between them seemed to be taking on a life of its own without any encouragement from him.

Or, apparently, from her.

Even so, the smile on her lips seemed to burrow right into his gut, grazing his chest as well.

"Nice to know," she commented.

He had no idea what to make of her response or, for that matter, of the way this whole afternoon had made him feel.

There was no denying that she was having some kind of effect on him. That alone surprised him. He would have bet any amount of money that he *was* dead inside. That, as with a scorched earth policy, nothing inside of him could possibly ever flourish.

But when he was around Catherine, he felt definite stirrings. He felt a quickening of his gut that he just couldn't—or maybe wouldn't—pin down.

It was easier, he told himself, just to drop the whole thing.

Easier said than done.

As with the scent of new blossoms in the spring, he found that thoughts of Catherine insisted on lingering in his mind, popping up to tease him when he was least prepared.

The last time he had felt even remotely this way was when he and Ren—

He blocked the rest of the thought. This was neither the time nor the place. He'd deal with it later, he told himself.

"So," Catherine said, making the single word sound like an announcement, "where would you like to go to eat, Cody?"

He didn't eat out much, certainly not as much as the average man—unless sitting by an open campfire could be called eating out. Consequently, he didn't know the names of many restaurants in town.

"The Hitching Post still closed?" he asked her. The last he'd heard, it had shut down for repairs, but he couldn't remember exactly when that was. If something didn't affect his basic way of life and the ranch, he usually didn't pay attention to it.

She nodded. "I'm afraid so. How about DJ's Rib Shack?" she suggested. "The food there is really good. I think you might like it. And DJ might be willing to give us a break on the price of dinner." She was only partially teasing.

As far as he knew, there was only one reason for that. "You know DJ?" he asked as he followed Catherine out of the shop.

It was such a fact of life for her that she'd forgotten other people might not know.

"Sure."

Catherine paused to engage the lock on the front door. She left it unlocked during the day, but somehow, since there was merchandise in the shop, she felt that leaving the door unlocked was like issuing a challenge to the universe. She wasn't quite brave enough to risk that sort of thing. Not when everything she owned was tied up in the shop.

"The Cliftons and the Traubs are old family friends," she told Cody, then looked at him as she slipped the keys into her pocket. "Why?" The way he's asked made her think that there was a connection between the two men. "You know DJ, too?"

"Just in passing," he answered. And it had been years since he'd last seen the younger man. "I went to high school with Dax, his older brother."

The moment he said that, he suddenly remembered that Dax had gotten engaged to Allaire around the exact same time that he had gotten engaged to Renee.

But talking about it would only wind up opening up the wounds again and maybe it was time to finally try to let them start to heal.

There was something he wasn't saying, Catherine thought as she walked with Cody toward his truck. She could feel it.

Catherine was tempted to prod him a little. But she

knew she really shouldn't. Whatever he was holding back, if he wanted her to know, he'd tell her. She had to be satisfied with that.

It wasn't easy.

Rolling the matter over in her mind, Catherine stopped just short of the truck and turned toward Cody. "Would you rather not go to the Rib Shack?" she asked. "We could go somewhere else or maybe pick up something at the General Store and I could whip up dinner for us in the shop." She'd done it a couple of times for herself when she'd stayed late. "There's a hot plate in the storage room and I could—"

He knew where she was going with this and she didn't need to make the offer, although the fact that she did in deference to what she thought were his feelings impressed him.

Still, he shook his head, dismissing her offer. "You worked enough today," he told her. "DJ's Rib Shack'll do just fine."

"They make better ribs than I do," she admitted.

"I doubt it."

He was probably just being polite, Catherine thought. Even so, the words warmed her heart.

Chapter Seven

DJ's Rib Shack was a popular restaurant, part of a chain of barbecue restaurants founded by DJ Traub. This particular one was located on the ground floor of the Thunder Canyon Resort and, because of its location, it saw more than its share of foot traffic. Business was always brisk at the Rib Shack but somehow, in Catherine's experience, there always seemed to be enough seating available so that she could get a table anytime she dropped by.

The atmosphere was boisterous and loud and patrons found that they had to sit close to one another when speaking. Otherwise, parts of their conversations were swallowed up by the noise. As for ambiance, it had the feel of simpler times about it. The walls were covered with old sepia-toned photographs of ranches and cowboys from eras gone by.

As Cody followed Catherine through the maze of

tables, while an animated hostess led the way to their table, he could only think to himself that this was definitely *not* a place to bring a date for the first time. Brightly lit and friendly, there was absolutely nothing romantic about the setting. This was a place where friends came to talk about a game that was played down to the wire and good old boys came to chew the fat and talk about their glory days.

Embarrassment over his earlier misunderstanding took another bite out of him, but Cody kept his thoughts stoically under wraps.

The table the hostess brought them to was practically in the center of the main room.

"You have a clear view of everything," the woman enthused. Cody merely nodded.

Waiting for Catherine to take her seat first, Cody slid in opposite her. The hostess presented them each with a menu before she withdrew.

Catherine didn't bother opening hers as she looked around and took in the atmosphere. She seemed to brighten visibly right in front of him, as if the accompanying noise recharged her somehow.

"It's busy tonight," Cody commented.

That was nothing new. "It's like this every night, or so I hear," she told him. When Cody made no reply, Catherine looked at him, curious. "This isn't your first time here, is it?"

Cody shrugged carelessly. Removing his Stetson, he placed the hat on the side of the table where a third diner might have sat. "I don't eat out," he told her.

She expected him to tag on the word *much*. When he didn't, not wanting him to feel awkward, she said, "I hardly do, either. But I really like to." She grinned.

"Best part of eating out is that there're no dishes or pots and pans to wash afterwards."

"You could cut down on the number by making everything in one pan and then just eating out of it," he said matter-of-factly.

Was that how he took his meals? That sounded so lonely. Catherine suddenly realized that her mouth had dropped open. She quickly closed it. Recovering, she told him, "I'd say that you need to eat out more than I do."

What he needed, he couldn't help thinking, was a way to talk his sister into leaving that good-for-nothing, controlling husband of hers so she could go back to being the happy young woman he remembered.

"Don't know if *need*'s the right word, but I'll admit that the change of pace is kinda nice," he said, looking directly at Catherine.

What was nicer, he thought, was having someone to talk to while he ate. He hadn't realized that he'd missed that as much as he did until just now.

A waitress came to take their orders. That they were having barbecue ribs was a foregone conclusion. It was just a matter of how much and what they wanted to drink that had to be settled on.

"Catherine, it *is* you. I haven't seen you around for a bit."

The pleased greeting came from someone just behind him. Cody shifted in his chair in time to see DJ Traub lean over the table and warmly take Catherine's hands in his.

"How's everyone at home?" DJ asked. "All well, I hope. What are you all doing with yourselves?"

Catherine slanted a quick glance at Cody to see if

this interruption bothered him. But he didn't seem to mind the intrusion, which pleased her.

"Everyone's well," she told DJ, slowly reclaiming her hands. "Calista's getting married and I'm about to reopen the old Tattered Saddle under a new name with new old merchandise. Why don't you and your wife come by to the grand opening next Friday?" she invited him.

She'd talked her brother into putting up flyers around town, but the personal touch never hurt. The more word spread about the reopening, the better her chances were of getting more customers to come to the shop.

"We'll be sure to do that," DJ promised. "I'm sure that Allaire will find something she likes, she always does." He grinned at her. "She can be your first customer."

"I'm afraid that Cody's already beaten her to that," Catherine said with a laugh, gesturing at Cody.

When she said the name, DJ glanced toward the man sitting at the table for the first time. Recognition suddenly flashed in his eyes.

"Cody?" he repeated. He asked uncertainly, "Cody Overton?"

"Yeah, that's me," Cody replied without any sort of fanfare.

DJ made up for it for both of them. Grasping Cody's hand, he pumped it up and down enthusiastically several times.

"How the hell are you?" he cried with genuine pleasure. "I haven't seen you since—well, forever, I guess." Not content to just let it go at that, DJ did his best to try to pinpoint the time. "High school, wasn't it?"

Cody nodded. "That's about right." Debating with himself for a minute or so, he asked the question that was on his mind. "Did I hear you say something about bringing Allaire?"

Ordinarily, he didn't pry into other people's lives, but since DJ's brother Dax had gotten engaged to Allaire at the same time that he had slipped an engagement ring on Renee's finger, it made him wonder how the other couple was faring. Had DJ taken to escorting his older brother's wife around?

Nodding, DJ said, "Yes, you did. Allaire's my wife." The surprised look in Cody's eyes was impossible to miss. Explanations were apparently in order. "I guess you didn't hear. Dax and Allaire divorced. Dax got married again and he's really happy this time, so things worked out for the best for everyone," he assured his newest patron. His words echoed back at him just as he remembered hearing the news about Cody's wife's untimely death. "I never had a chance to tell you how really sorry I was to hear about Renee," he said solemnly to Cody.

"Thanks," Cody replied crisply. He really didn't want to get into that now. Not here. Actually, not anywhere. Especially not around the woman sitting opposite him at the table. He closed the topic by saying, "She would have been happy for you. She always thought you had a thing for Allaire."

DJ laughed softly, not bothering to deny what had been an open secret to everyone but his older brother. "I always said Renee was a class act." He placed a hand on Cody's shoulder. "Well, I've got to get back to mingling," he told them. "Really great seeing you again,

Cody. Order anything you like," he told them, beginning to back away. "Dinner's on me."

"Oh, no, that's all right," Catherine began to protest.

Already moving on to another table, DJ paused for just a moment longer. "One thing you're going to be learning, Catie, is that nobody argues with the owner. That's one of the perks of *being* the owner," he told her with a wink.

The next moment he was gone, absorbed by the din and the crowd.

"Well, I guess that means I still owe you a dinner out," Catherine said, leaning forward so that Cody could hear her.

"You don't owe me anything," Cody told her briskly. "You gave me that coin purse to send to Caroline, remember?"

The smile on her lips told him that she remembered, all right. "How did that work out, anyway?" Catherine asked. "Did your sister receive her gift in time?"

He remembered the call that morning and struggled to block the anger that accompanied the memory. "Yeah, it got there, all right."

He didn't sound very happy about it. Not that she expected him to do handsprings; she knew better than that. But she had seen him several notches happier on a couple of occasions.

"Something wrong with it?" she asked, wondering if the gift had met with an accident while en route or if his sister ultimately hadn't liked the purse.

"No, nothing was wrong with it." Why was she asking? He was fairly certain that he hadn't given anything away with his expression. "As a matter of fact, Caroline called this morning to thank me for it, so I guess

I should pass that thanks on to you since you were the one who insisted I take it."

"Okay, there's nothing wrong with *it,* but there *is* something wrong," Catherine insisted. "I can see it in your eyes."

No, she couldn't, he thought in protest. He always kept a tight rein on his emotions. "Just the lighting," he finally said with a shrug.

Catherine looked at him pointedly. "You know, if someone had asked me, I would have bet money that you didn't lie. I guess I would have lost that bet, huh?" There was a look of disappointment on her face.

Cody opened his mouth to protest, to insist that he wasn't lying, but the words never rose to his lips. Instead, he sighed in resignation.

He supposed there was no point in denying it any longer. "It's just that I wish she'd wake up."

He was going to have to elaborate on that one. "Come again?"

Instead, Cody just repeated what he'd just said. "I wish she'd wake up."

"About what?" she coaxed.

For an unguarded moment, anger flashed in his green eyes. "About that damned worthless piece of garbage she's married to."

Watching him intently, Catherine came to her own conclusions. For Cody to say that with such feeling… Only one of two things could have prompted those words from him.

She took a guess. "Does he abuse her?"

He laughed shortly. It was the sound of complete frustration. "She won't tell me—"

"But you suspect it." The waitress returned to refill their glasses. Catherine paused, waiting for the woman to leave again before she continued. "Why?" she pressed the second the waitress turned away. Was Cody just being overprotective or was there something concrete he was basing all this on?

"Why?" he echoed almost in contempt, but his ire was directed at the man who wasn't there. "Because every time I talk to her, Caroline sounds like she's afraid of her own shadow. She keeps her voice low, like she's afraid he'll overhear her. It's not that she's saying anything bad, I just get the feeling she's not supposed to talk to *anyone*. And she goes along with that," he lamented angrily.

Taking a breath, he continued, "She never used to be like that. She was a fighter who didn't take anything from anyone. At least—" he scrubbed his hand over his face "—she used to be like that. It's as if the bum just sucked out her soul and left this quaking shell in its wake." There was bitterness in his voice. "She called today to thank me for remembering her. She was hardly on the phone for two minutes when I heard him bellowing for her. I could almost *hear* her jump. She said she had to go and then hung up before I could say anything else to her."

That did sound like someone who was being at least mentally abused, if not physically as well.

"Well, if she were my sister and I really thought she was being abused by her husband, I'd drive up to wherever she was and *make* her come back with me until I could sort everything out—and meanwhile have the bastard arrested for domestic abuse."

The answer, coming from her, surprised him. He

studied Catherine's face for a long moment, his eyes searching hers.

She meant what she'd just said, Cody realized. She might look like she'd be easygoing, a person who just floated along with things, but she really did have more than her share of spunk—just the way he'd initially thought.

He liked that.

Liked the fact that she'd also just displayed that she had a very strong sense of family. "And that's what you'd do if it was your sister?" he asked.

She nodded with enthusiasm, then said, "Hell, I'd do it if it was *your* sister." Which brought her to another question. "You want me to go see her, talk to her for you?"

There was just no end to the surprises with this woman. And with each discovery, he found himself liking her more and more.

"You'd really do that?" he pressed.

There was no hesitation—or any bravado for that matter. Just a simple conviction. "Sure, if you think I could help. People should always be willing to help other people in trouble," she told him simply. "So," she said after a moment's pause, "do you want me to go see her, talk to her?"

"No," he said. Not that he wasn't grateful, but this was his battle to fight, not hers. "Besides, you've got a grand opening to get ready for," he reminded her. "I'll give Caroline a little longer to come around and start acting more like her old self." And then he shrugged. "Who knows, maybe I'm just overreacting. I never did like that guy," he freely admitted. And then he lowered his voice so that he was almost talking to himself. Catherine leaned in even closer. "And to be honest, I do feel a little responsible for her being with him."

There was only one interpretation as far as she could see. "You set them up when you didn't like the guy?" Catherine asked.

But even as she put the question to him, she couldn't imagine him doing anything like that.

"No, nothing like that," he said quickly. "It's just that I think she married Rory because she didn't want to be alone." He saw by the question in her eyes that he had some backtracking to do.

"Our parents were killed in a hit-and-run accident when I was eighteen. After I got married, my sister suddenly found herself all alone in a house that had once held four people. She felt abandoned, and when Rory asked her to marry him, I guess she just jumped at it, because she needed someone of her own. She thought Rory was that someone," he concluded with a deep, disgruntled sigh.

Cody usually just kept everything under wraps and part of him was really surprised that he was unloading this way to another human being. But there was just something about *this* particular human being that seemed to draw the words out of him.

"I should have insisted she come live with us. Renee thought it would be a good idea. I went along with it, but I have to admit I was a little relieved when Caroline turned the offer down. I was being selfish." When he looked up at her, Catherine could see the guilt in his eyes. "I wanted to be alone with Renee. I felt like we were still on our honeymoon and I really wanted that feeling to last."

She'd *known* there was a softer side to this man.

The fact that he could agonize over something he felt he could have done differently—rather than just shrug it off—proved it.

"You weren't being selfish," she insisted, putting her hand on top of his, unconsciously forming an unspoken bond. "You were just being a newlywed. There's nothing wrong with that." She found it touching and sensitive, but she had a feeling that if she said anything to that effect, it would only irritate him, so for the time being, she kept that part to herself.

Instead, she painted a slightly broader stroke. "The fact that you even *offered* to take your sister in shows that your heart was in the right place."

A lot of good that did Caroline now, Cody thought darkly as guilt scratched away at him. He could tell just by her tone and the things that Catherine was saying that the young woman was really trying hard to absolve him of that.

He did his best to pay her back by attempting to lighten the mood. "Are you always this Pollyannaish?" he asked her.

"Always," she told him. "I find that it helps get me through the day—and I've got a feeling that my positive attitude is going to come in real handy once I open Real Vintage Cowboy for business."

Catherine was well aware that she had a big, uphill battle before her. Most new businesses failed before the end of their first year.

She didn't intend to.

"The what?" he asked, realizing that his mind had drifted off for a second even though his eyes had been all but nailed down on one view.

Catherine.

He caught himself looking at her as if he hadn't seen her before. Was it just him or was she actually getting prettier as they sat here?

"The store," she reminded him tactfully. "Real Vintage Cowboy," she repeated. "That's the name I gave it, remember?"

"I do now," he admitted. His wince was exaggerated as he went on to ask her, "You sure you want to go with that name?"

She didn't understand why he didn't like it and she certainly wasn't about to be dissuaded from using it. She really liked the name she'd come up with. And he had been her inspiration.

"Yes, I'm sure I want to 'go with that name.' I named the store after this really grumpy cowboy I recently met," she told him, tongue in cheek. "And besides, I think it's very appropriate. They both seem to represent something that's a little old, a little new, a little reliable, a little unpredictable." Catherine was looking at him pointedly as she went over the various diametrically opposing traits she'd witnessed him display.

"You get all that out of a single name, huh?" he marveled with an echo of a laugh punctuating his question.

Catherine nodded. "Yup. Pretty good, don't you think?"

"Haven't given it that much thought," he lied. "I just think it's a mouthful, that's all."

She leaned her head on her upturned palm and asked, "Okay, I'll bite. What would *you* call it?"

He thought for a second, then said, "The Place."

She waited for more. There wasn't any. "'The Place'? That's it?" she asked, stunned.

He didn't see the problem. "Yeah. I figure that's enough."

Catherine shook her head. "Good thing it's my store and not yours" She laughed softly. The look in her eyes reinforced the sound.

It took Cody more than a couple of seconds to rouse himself before he could go back to eating his dinner. Not that there was much room left in his stomach, not after it had all but tightened into a knot the way it had just now.

Chapter Eight

All through dinner, Catherine had been trying to find a way to broach the subject that DJ had inadvertently introduced when he'd stopped by earlier. But here she was, more than halfway finished with the meal and the question still sat there in her mind like an impenetrable fortress that had no visible point of access.

Finally, she decided that if she wanted to know anything, she was just going to have to leap into the center of it like a paratrooper jumping out of an airplane.

"Renee was your wife?"

She kept her tone mild, upbeat. Even so, she saw Cody's shoulders instantly become rigid. When he raised his head to look at her, she found that she was looking into the eyes of a man who had completely closed himself off again.

Well, you started this. Get on with it, Catherine silently ordered herself. *There's no turning back for you anymore.*

"Yes." The single word sounded heavy with emotion, as if he was telling her that if she continued down this path, it was at her own risk.

Catherine pushed onward. She pressed her lips together, summoning courage and hoping that her words didn't wind up reopening any wounds.

"DJ said he was sorry about what happened." Her throat almost felt as if it was raw as she quietly asked the key question that had been preying on her mind, "What did happen?"

His face was utterly expressionless as he answered, "Renee died."

Catherine's breath immediately evaporated from her lungs. She wasn't exactly sure what she'd expected Cody to say. Something along the lines, she realized, that the woman, unable to put up with his sullenness any longer, had left him.

This put an entirely new spin on the matter.

She could feel her heart quickening as it overflowed with sympathy. "Oh—"

He'd heard that sound before, that sharp intake of breath that occurred before the woman who'd uttered the single word suddenly launched into an emotion-dripping speech aimed at helping him heal—and at obtaining his undying gratitude and loyalty in the process.

Ain't gonna happen, he thought with a vengeance.

Served him right for thinking that Catherine was different from the others.

Cody cut her off before Catherine could say anything further. His eyes narrowed as he asked, "You're not going to turn into one of those women who feels sorry for 'the poor helpless widower,' are you?"

Catherine could almost hear the sneer in his voice. "Well, I *am* sorry for your loss and for the grief you've obviously gone through," she told him.

She saw that Cody had moved back his chair and realized that he was getting up to leave. She talked faster, hoping to get him to change his mind with her words. It was all she had since she had no intentions of attempting to hog-tie him or throw herself in his path, blocking his exit.

"But I hardly see you as a 'helpless' anything. You're obviously fending for yourself. You've got that ranch of yours where I hear that you're making a decent living training quarter horses."

Almost against his will, Cody lowered himself back down onto his chair, then moved it back until his legs were squarely under the table again. But he wasn't completely settled in.

Yet.

His eyes narrowed again as he studied her. "How do you know I train quarter horses?" he asked. "Or that I even have a ranch, much less that I'm making—how did you put it—a 'decent living' at it?"

"Word gets around," Catherine told him matter-of-factly.

Especially if you ask, she added silently. She'd had her older brother, Craig, find out a few basic things about Cody for her, which he did just to make sure that she was safe around "this character," as he referred to Cody.

But Cody didn't need to know that part—especially since, she had a feeling, it would probably make him withdraw into whatever shell he was in the habit of residing in. The Cody Craig had told her about wasn't generally regarded as a "social" creature.

Cody pinned her with a long, penetrating look. She met it head-on, her chin raised stubbornly. She was waiting for him to *say* something.

"People don't spend time talking about me." He all but growled out the words.

"You'd be surprised," she countered cheerfully. "This is a small town. Not a heck of a whole lot to talk about *except* the people who come and go here. And you," she elaborated, "are tall—*really* tall—and you might not be 'dark,' but you do have this brooding air about you. That makes you just perfect for speculation and gossip from some people's point of view."

He resented people poking into his life, invading his privacy, but he supposed she did have a point. There were times when it seemed like gossip was the main thing that was produced in Thunder Canyon.

"Then you knew about Renee," he assumed out loud. And if she had, it suddenly occurred to him, why was she asking questions?

"No, I didn't," she maintained. "I wouldn't have asked you if I did. I don't go around inflicting pain on people, and I can see now that this talking about your late wife causes you a great deal of pain. I'm sorry, I didn't mean to open any old wounds."

He didn't like being seen as vulnerable—even when he was.

Unconsciously squaring his shoulders, he lowered his eyes to his meal, but he addressed the question Catherine had asked earlier and answered it more fully. "Renee came down with cancer. Fought it like a champion, but in the end, the damn disease won." There was a defiant look in his eyes when he raised them to hers again. "Anything else you want to know?"

"Yes," she answered. Then, as he visibly braced himself to be ready for whatever unintentionally painful question came out of her mouth, Catherine—an extremely serious expression on her face—asked, "You going to eat those?" She pointed to the fries he seemed to have abandoned on his plate as he'd turned his attention to the ribs he'd ordered.

"Yes, I am," he informed her. And then the formal tone he'd adopted slipped away as he added, "But I'll share 'em with you."

Catherine grinned. "Can't ask for anything more than that."

There was a challenge in the look he gave her. "Sure you can. Women always do."

"Maybe you haven't known enough women," she suggested.

"Maybe," he conceded.

Cody had to admit that he liked the way she held her ground and wasn't cowed or scared off by his somber reaction. He especially liked that her eyes hadn't filled with overwhelming pity when she'd heard about Renee. Maybe she really wasn't one of those women who felt they had an absolute obligation to fix every man they deemed was broken.

That alone made Catherine Clifton pretty unique in his book.

"You're right," he told her after several beats had gone by.

She waited until several more beats had slipped away. When Cody didn't elaborate on his initial statement, she felt that this time she was within her rights to press him.

"Right about what?"

He nodded at the spareribs on his plate, or rather at just the bare ribs since that was all that was left. "This *is* good. *Was* good," he amended.

"Never heard of anyone walking out of here dissatisfied," she told him, obviously pleased that he had decided to be straightforward with her and rescind his initial skepticism. There were men, she knew, who would rather go to their grave than to tell a woman that she was right and they were wrong.

She wasn't exactly sure why it pleased her so much that Cody didn't fall into that category, but it did.

"I guess DJ's doing well for himself," Cody commented after a bit.

She couldn't tell if Cody was envious of the younger man or not, then decided that the man she was getting to know wasn't the sort to harbor emotions such as jealousy or even envy. He seemed to be above that kind of petty behavior.

"He doesn't have any complaints," she answered. "But I think he counts himself luckier that he has Allaire in his life."

The moment she said it, Catherine immediately clamped her lips together. Because she knew that nothing meant as much to DJ as his wife, what she'd just said had come out without any hesitation. But once her words echoed back to her, Catherine realized that it had to seem to him that she was rubbing salt into his wounds.

"I'm sorry," she apologized haltingly, not sure how

to phrase this or even if she should just keep quiet altogether. "I shouldn't have said that."

"Why not?" Cody wanted to know. "It's true, isn't it?"

That wasn't the point. The point was that she'd accidentally seemed callous. "Yes, but—"

"If it's true, then there is no 'but.' What, you're afraid that what you just said will set off a fresh wave of pain in my gut?" he wanted to know. The laugh that emerged from his lips was harsh, without a single trace of humor in it. "I don't need to have to hear someone saying something for that to happen. The pain's there all the time, but I'm doing my damndest to finally make my peace with it."

"Well, I wasn't exactly helping the process—" she began before becoming bogged down in her apology. She wasn't really sure where to go from here.

He looked at her for another very long moment. So long that it seemed almost endless to her, but she didn't flinch, didn't look away. And then he finally spoke. "Oh, I don't know. Maybe you were. You certainly thought you were, bringing me out here."

She wasn't trying to be underhanded, she thought defensively. "I brought you out here just to say thank you," she reminded him.

"For that, all you had to do was just move your lips, not drive all the way over here." Then, because it did sound to him as if he was complaining, Cody amended his statement by saying, "But, to be fair, this did turn out to be a much nicer experience than I thought it was going to be."

Was that actually a compliment? Catherine looked

at the source of her inspiration uncertainly. "Just what was it that you were expecting?"

He lifted one shoulder in a vague half shrug. "Mediocre food at best and awkwardness."

Catherine couldn't help laughing. "Well, you certainly are honest."

He appeared surprised by the assessment and by the fact that his being that way would have caught this deceptively easygoing woman off guard. He was beginning to realize that she was pretty damn sharp.

"No point in being anything else," he told her matter-of-factly. Finished, he wiped his lips with his napkin then looked down thoughtfully at his plate. "You know, maybe I will have seconds."

Although he saw it quite by accident as he was looking around for their waitress, Cody caught the pleased look in Catherine's eyes. Caught it and found himself responding to it in ways he would have *sworn* on a stack of Bibles were all behind him.

Part of him thought he'd made a mistake when he'd changed his mind about leaving earlier. The part that was warming up, though, felt he would have made the mistake if he *had* picked up and left.

Right now, it was a toss-up which part was actually right.

The rest of the evening turned out to be even more fun than he'd thought possible. And it all had to do with something he'd told himself he no longer felt up to doing: socializing.

Several people he hadn't even given a thought to in the last eight years stopped by their table to greet him, exchange a few words and express their pleasure at seeing him "out and about again," something that had last occurred just before Renee had been diagnosed with cancer.

While he had never been one to crave company and had been more than content when it had been just Renee and him tucked away on his ranch, Cody'd found that interacting with some of their neighbors and Renee's friends had amounted to a fairly pleasant experience whenever it occurred.

In large measure, he'd done it for Renee because he knew that it pleased her to mingle like this. The same way it pleased her to help others whenever she could. It was just the kind of woman she was.

Selfless.

Being here with Catherine now brought all that back to him. But rather than overwhelm him with waves of unbearable sorrow, it seemed to pull him toward the present and away from the past.

And ever so slowly, it was beginning to make him feel that maybe, just maybe, there actually was a future for him after all.

Maybe it was a stretch to admit this, but if he was being honest—with himself if with no one else—he'd have to say that he was really enjoying this effervescent woman's company.

He was even enjoying listening to her share her plans for the shop with him. In a way, it was like listening to a child anticipating a visit from that iconic jolly old elf, Santa Claus.

Though Cody was fairly certain that this woman probably *wasn't* really as innocent as she seemed, Catherine did display an innocent, almost childlike exuberance when she talked about making a success of the shop she'd bought. He realized that she was really committed to that.

He caught himself thinking that he could listen to her talk about the shop for hours.

Which was, more or less, what he wound up doing.

As if suddenly becoming aware that she'd had gone on and on, dragging Cody into all her plans and hopes, Catherine's narrative came to an abrupt halt as she cried, "I've talked your ears off."

After they'd finally left the restaurant, Cody and she had driven back to the shop and then had gone on a long, leisurely stroll—to "walk off the calories."

At least that was the way that Catherine had put it, but he had a hunch that if those calories were actually falling away, they were doing so in what felt like complete slow motion.

The lengthy stroll came to an end right before the shop. It was where she'd decided to crash tonight in order to get an early start in the morning. When Catherine had bought the boarded-up store, she'd realized that there were two inhabitable floors directly above the ground floor. She'd decided to retain the second floor for herself, creating an office and a place to crash when she needed to. The third floor she wound up renting out to a woman who was working at the Gallatin Room as a part-time waitress/bartender.

In response to her protest that she'd talked his ears off, Cody quietly made a solemn show of touching first one ear, then the other.

"Nope," he deadpanned. "You didn't talk them off. Looks like they're both still there."

Her eyes widened as if she'd just been privy to a huge revelation. And in a way, she was.

"You've got a sense of humor," she cried in delighted surprise, then smiled. "That's a really good thing to know for future reference."

He didn't see why, but he had a feeling that asking might get him even more deeply embroiled in a scenario he didn't understand. Instead, he merely shrugged carelessly. "Didn't know that my having or not having a sense of humor was a point of concern."

"It's just better to have one than not have one," Catherine told him. She really couldn't relate to someone who didn't have a sense of humor. "Well, I'm really glad you let me drag you out," she said, putting out her hand to him.

Saying that was her way of letting Cody maintain his solemn facade. In her heart she knew that if Cody hadn't wanted to come along, not even dynamite would have compelled him to go out to DJ's.

Her smile widened as she fixed it on Cody. "I had a great time."

He inclined his head, covering her slender hand with his own. "Yeah, it wasn't bad," he conceded.

Emulating a heroine in a melodrama, Catherine placed the back of her free hand to her forehead, like a woman subject to "vapors."

"Please, such heady praise. I'm not sure I can handle it." And then the sound of her laughter—light and melodic—filled the still night air like silver bells. "Don't forget, I'm counting on you being there at the grand opening next week," she said, wanting to remind him before he left.

"I'll be there," Cody promised.

Okay, this was the part, he told himself, where he slipped his hand from hers and walked off to his truck.

The only problem was, his hand wasn't slipping from hers. He was still holding it, still looking down into her mesmerizing, upturned brown eyes.

Still feeling all sorts of things going on in the pit of his stomach. Things that had nothing to do with the meal he'd just had and everything to do with the woman he'd had it with.

Before he knew it, rather than releasing her hand and turning away to walk to his vehicle, Cody found that he'd pulled Catherine *to* him.

When he finally let go of her hand, it was because he needed both of his to frame her face.

His heart was suddenly doing a fair imitation of a race car's engine. He felt it launch into triple time as he anticipated what he knew was coming next.

With his breath lodged in his throat, Cody felt like some damn teenager. Even so, he framed Catherine's face between his hands, inclined his head more than a little in order to reach her lips—and then he kissed her.

A second later, all hell suddenly broke loose, threatening the stability of the immediate world.

It certainly threatened his.

Chapter Nine

What the hell was he doing? Had he completely lost his mind?

Faintly whispered questions involving the condition of his sanity assaulted Cody from all sides as the kiss that had surprised him just as much as it did the woman who was on the receiving end of it deepened and grew in intensity.

Cody had no answers to those questions, nor could he spare the energy to formulate any. Every molecule in his body was entirely focused was on what was happening right at this moment.

The longer he kissed Catherine, the greater his *need* to kiss her became until Cody felt as if he was being pulled into some bottomless vortex where the only thing that truly mattered was this woman and the feeling generated between them.

Cody dropped his hands from her face and used

them to draw her closer to him. So close that it seemed as if they were melding into one another, two halves of a very unique whole.

He really wasn't sure where he left off and Catherine began.

It didn't matter.

Damn, but she made his blood rush and his head spin. Not only that, but he was fairly certain that there was very little air left in his lungs. That, too, didn't matter.

Nothing mattered but this moment, this feeling. This woman.

Caught completely off guard, there wasn't even half a second to spare for surprise to register. What *did* register was pleasure. Absolutely, profound, exquisite pleasure.

Catherine had had her suspicions that this loner of a cowboy could make her blood heat to almost boiling and now she knew that she'd been right.

But this wasn't the time for any triumphant feelings or even the time to think.

Because she couldn't.

Couldn't, she was fairly certain, even answer the simplest of questions because her brain had just short-circuited in the intense heat that had flashed through her like a raw current from a lightning bolt. All she really knew was that she was grateful Cody was holding her as closely as he was because she was sure that her entire body had taken on the composition of a liquid.

More specifically, the composition of molten lava.

Cody knew he had to step back and step back *now* because even five more seconds like this and the whole situation would be completely out of his hands and *way* out of control.

Even now, all he really wanted to do was take Catherine inside her store and make love to her until they were both light years beyond exhausted.

But there would be consequences if he did that. Consequences he wasn't sure he was ready to deal with.

So, with more effort than he'd thought would be necessary, more effort than he'd ever had to employ with anyone before, Cody forced himself to pull back.

Even after he did, his heart continued slamming against his rib cage like a newly incarcerated prisoner trying to break free of the iron bars he found looming before him.

Hell.

He could still taste Catherine on his lips. The temptation to take her back into his arms was damn near overwhelming.

Cody looked down into her dazed, upturned face. His breathing had yet to return to normal. "If you're waiting for me to say I'm sorry, you've got a long wait ahead of you," he warned.

Catherine moved her head from side to side—slowly so as not to fall over. "I don't want you to say you're sorry," she whispered.

He took in a deep breath, nodding his approval even though he was uncertain exactly what it was he was approving. Right now, confusion ruled and he wasn't even sure which direction was up and which was down.

Kissing her had turned his world on its ear.

"Good," he finally declared. He pulled his Stetson down farther until the brim all but obscured his eyebrows and hid his eyes. "'Cause I don't know why the hell I just did that, but I know I'm not sorry that I did," he emphasized.

And then, just like that, Cody turned on his heel and went back to his vehicle.

Catherine stood exactly where she was, watching the truck as it grew smaller and smaller before disappearing around the corner.

The crisp September air had a definite chill in it, whispering of winter's nearness. She didn't feel it. At this very moment, she was aware of being extremely hot to the point that had she been dressed in shorts and a tank top, she would have still been radiating heat from every pore in her body.

Catherine did her best to think, to review the events as they had transpired, and found that she was going to have to delay that until a later time. Her brain had temporarily ceased functioning and gave no indication that it was about to kick in again.

At least not for a while.

Hugging her shawl to her, Catherine went inside the shop, encased in the moment and a contentment she'd never experienced before.

Her mouth curved. It looked like her vintage cowboy was certainly full of surprises.

"Anything I can do to help?"

The deep voice rumbled into her consciousness, making her jump. Catherine looked in the direction of the voice—although there was really no need to. She knew who was asking the question because the sound of his voice had hardly left her head these last few days.

Cody had been on her mind and in her dreams ever

since that life-altering kiss in front of her shop the other evening.

She'd tried to busy herself with plans and bury herself in work that was all targeted for her grand opening. But even that wasn't enough to drown out his presence.

Catherine was beginning to doubt that anything was.

"Help?" Catherine repeated the word as if it was completely foreign to her.

"Yeah. To get ready for that grand opening, or re-opening, you're holding for this store." He could see how much making the store a success seemed to mean to her and if that was what made her happy, then he wanted to ensure that the grand opening was going to be the success that she was hoping for. "Thought you might need an extra hand or two," he added as an afterthought.

Just then, the door to the rear storage area opened and three people came in, two young women and a man, all of them looking enough like one another—and Catherine—to make him realize that they had to be related.

Seeing all of them here made him feel slightly out of place, so he lifted a shoulder in a vague, dismissive shrug.

"Or not," he tossed in. "Looks to me like you've already got enough hands."

He was going to leave, Catherine realized in alarm. Without thinking, she grabbed hold of his arm, her survival instincts kicking in before she could stop herself with any logical thought process.

"Never enough hands," she told him, recovering. And then she smiled up at Cody. "I could use you for some of the heavy lifting." It was the first thing that came to her mind and she felt that it might appeal to the machismo in him.

Cody arched one very quizzical eyebrow as he looked at her. Almost everything around them in the shop looked as if it weighed at least a ton. He was strong, but he wasn't *that* strong.

"Just what is it that you want lifted?" he asked suspiciously.

"Moved actually," she amended, pointing to an armoire that she'd spent hours working on in order to return it to its original shine. "I thought that might look better against the far wall."

Cody regarded the heavy piece of furniture. "I don't know. I think it might get more attention out in the open right where it is. The customers can't help but see it when they walk in," he added for good measure.

"Okay." Catherine nodded, considering his argument. "I'm open to advice. If you think it'll be noticed faster this way," she allowed, "then we'll keep it right where it is." She flashed a grin at him, guessing what he was probably thinking. "Don't worry, I've got smaller things to move."

"Never doubted that you did," he quipped. "Just point them out and tell me where you want them."

"Where do you want us?" Craig asked. He glanced at his watch. C.C. and Cecilia had dragged him here to give Catherine moral support. "I don't have that much time to give."

"So you've said four or five times already," C.C. cracked.

"But who's counting," Cecilia, ever the peacemaker, chimed in. She made sure to suppress the grin that wanted to rise to her lips.

"I've got another batch of flyers," Catherine said, reaching underneath the counter.

After pulling them out she stacked the pile beside the old-fashioned cash register she'd dug up after an extensive search. She wanted to be able to ring up sales on something that was in keeping with the general motif of the shop.

"Of course you do," C.C. murmured, offering her older sister a tolerant smile.

Catherine divided the flyers into three equal batches, then handed a stack to each of her siblings. "Put them up wherever you see an empty space," she instructed.

Cecilia looked at the flyers she had in her arms. "You mean there's actually wall space left that doesn't have one of these things pasted on it?" She'd already been recruited to hang up flyers earlier in the week.

"Lots of places," Catherine assured her sister. Then, in case one of them wanted to challenge her statement, she added, "I checked."

"Well then, let's get to it, shall we?" Cecilia proposed to her younger sister and older brother, tongue in cheek. She paused to salute Catherine, then left the shop with C.C., ready to post flyers wherever she found an open spot.

Craig was a little slower in his follow-through. Instead, he carefully scrutinized the man his sister had asked him to look into.

The man had to represent her newest project, Craig decided. Once a caregiver, always a caregiver, he thought. And from what she'd had him find out about Cody Overton, the man was a project that would keep her busy for quite some time to come. He hadn't had the easiest life and it had made him distant and reclusive.

Catherine, he had a hunch, was going to try to change that.

"You're not giving a batch to your friend?" Craig asked, nodding at Cody.

"I've got other plans for him," Catherine told him, sparing Cody a quick, decisive glance.

I just bet you do, Craig thought.

But out loud he made no quip, saying instead, "Then I guess I'd better get going." He glanced in Cody's direction. He was still undecided whether he liked what he saw or not. As the oldest, he felt responsible for all his sisters.

"See you around," Craig said to his sister's project. With that, Craig, armed with an armload of fliers, made his way to the front door and left.

Cody took off his hat, laying it carefully on the counter, then rolled up his sleeves one at a time. "What did you have in mind?" he asked, nodding toward the furnishings.

Catherine pointed out a group of bookcases she'd picked up at an estate sale. She had painted them an antique white when the initial old color had defied restoration.

"I'd like those all brought over there." She pointed to a spot that could easily be viewed through the front window.

As Cody moved the bookcases one by one, she debated whether or not to say anything. But after a moment, she decided that her truthfulness was an asset in this case. She had a feeling Cody could spot a phony— even a well-intentioned phony—the proverbial mile away. "I wasn't sure if I'd see you here again."

Cody stopped moving the bookcase and looked at

her, surprised by her admission and that she'd thought it in the first place. After all, they weren't exactly sophomores in high school anymore.

At this point, he was beginning to doubt that he had ever been that young.

"You mean after I kissed you the other night?" he asked.

When he said it out loud like that, it sounded pretty foolish. But she'd started this, so she had no choice but to answer him.

"Well, yes," she admitted.

He couldn't read her expression. It had been a long time since he'd felt the need to try to second-guess what another person—a woman, specifically—was thinking. He'd gotten rusty at it and for once, Catherine's face was not completely animated.

Maybe he made her uncomfortable, Cody thought. "You want me to leave?"

No! But she knew she couldn't say that, at least, not with the kind of emphasis that had just echoed through her head. It might make him feel hemmed in or smothered. God, but men were so hard to read.

So instead, she forced herself to ask a question. "Do you want to?"

"It's not about me," he said pointedly. "It's about you. What *you* want. So, do you want me to go?" he asked again.

Her mother had always said that a lady never allows her true feelings for a man to show completely, especially not at the outset. Her mother said that it made a woman look too needy, too accessible, and she lost the air of mystery that was her main bargaining chip.

But all those rules, it seemed to Catherine, were for

games and she didn't think that something as important as a person's feelings should be treated as some
sort of game.

So, drawing her courage to her—and desperately
trying to still her nerves—Catherine answered Cody
truthfully. "No, I don't. As a matter of fact, I was afraid
that you wouldn't come back at all, not even for Real
Vintage Cowboy's grand opening."

"Why would you think that?" he wanted to know.
He was really trying to understand her reasoning. "Was
the kiss really that bad?"

"No," she whispered, afraid that if she spoke any
louder, her voice might quake and give her away. "It
was that good."

Cody stared at her as he took the news in. He
wanted to kiss her again. Nothing else had occupied
his thoughts since he'd walked away and left her on the
doorstep that night.

The pragmatic side of him had wanted to kiss her
again to make certain that what he'd experienced wasn't
just a fluke. The free-spirited side of him had wanted
to kiss Catherine again just to kiss her again.

He smiled then. One of his rare, starting in the middle and radiating out to all corners smiles that instantly
warmed her and went on to warm the room around
her as well.

Instead of saying anything, Cody touched her chin
with the tip of his finger and raised it just a little, tilt-
ing her head back.

And then he brushed his lips over hers.

At first lightly, then again, and again, each time with
more intensity, more fervor than the last until the kiss
from the other evening was revisited in its full intensity.

She was sinking again—and it was exhilarating, she couldn't help thinking, grasping on to Cody's arms to anchor herself as well as to give herself leverage. Leverage she needed in order to rise up on her toes and absorb even more of the kiss than she had the first time around.

Slowly, as Catherine found herself falling into the kiss completely, she moved her hands up until they were around Cody's neck. Her heart pounding, she held on for dear life.

"Is that some new way to move furniture that I don't know about?"

The deep voice splintered the moment.

Her heart pounding madly, Catherine pulled away from Cody to see that her brother had returned and was standing there looking at them.

Pushing both her embarrassment and her annoyance over Craig turning up like this aside, Catherine finally found her voice and said, "It's a new technique we're trying out."

Cody felt the corners of his mouth curving in amusement. Who knew the woman could be a feisty little hellcat to this degree?

He was finding more and more about her to like each time he was around her.

"How's that working out for you?" Craig deadpanned.

"Just fine, thanks for asking." Catherine redirected the line of questioning to focus on him, not on her or Cody. "What are you doing back so soon? You couldn't have distributed all those flyers already." She looked pointedly at the stack of posters he was holding in his hand.

"Sharp as a tack, this one," Craig commented to

Cody before answering her question. "I forgot my tape." He picked up a roll from the counter and deliberately held it up for her inspection as if it was exhibit A in a trial. "I'll be on my way now," he announced. "So you two can get back to trying out your new 'technique' again."

And with that, Craig left the shop for a second time, closing the door behind him.

Humor echoed in Cody's voice as he said, "Think I might get to like him," just before he pulled her back into his arms.

Catherine never got a chance to comment on his assessment of her brother. Cody's mouth had found hers again with no trouble at all.

The rest was a blur.

Chapter Ten

Without meaning to, Cody had upended her life to such a degree that it became increasingly difficult for her to focus on anything else except for the man who had inspired her shop's new name.

Still, she *did* have a lot of work left to do and the work was not about to do itself. There was a deadline breathing down her neck. The flyers were out and the grand opening of Real Vintage Cowboy was set for Friday at two, so the shop absolutely, positively had to be ready by then.

That meant that there was still an overwhelming amount of work get done.

She had endless checklists connected to that goal running through her head, and at times, Catherine felt as if she was going in four different directions all at the same time. Each time she started doing one thing, she thought of something else she needed to attend to, another estate sale she wanted to monitor on her laptop, another piece she thought could be improved upon, et cetera.

Consequently, she found herself doing six things at once, completing none because yet *another* thing demanded her attention.

Catherine began to feel as if she was wearing out from the inside out.

Cody put in as much time as he could spare away from his ranch and the quarter horses he was training. He was lucky in that the two ranch hands who worked for him had been with him since the beginning and knew the routine that was involved as well as he did.

For the first time since Renee's passing, he found himself actually wanting to leave the ranch rather than using any excuse to hide there. Things, he thought, were definitely changing for him.

And Catherine was the reason behind the change.

Watching her move quickly about the shop brought to mind the image of a propelled ball bearing that had been released in an old-fashioned pinball machine. He shook his head, growing exhausted by proxy.

"You might want to just finish one thing at a time," he finally suggested.

"I would if I could, but there's always something else I realize I've forgotten to do," Catherine told him as she raced by Cody on her way to the storage room.

When Cody suddenly blocked her path and took hold of her shoulders, she came to a skidding, abrupt halt. Confused, the look she shot at Cody was ripe with impatience.

Was he trying to make some kind of point?

Now?

"What?" she bit off, then flushed because she realized that she must have sounded like some kind of a shrew. "What?" she repeated, saying the word a little more softly. In both cases, however, her impatience all but vibrated through the word. She didn't have time for this. She still had eight hundred and ninety-seven things to do before Friday, or at least that was the way it felt to her.

"Slow down a little," he advised in the same tone he used to gentle an agitated horse.

Easy for him to say. His success or failure wasn't riding on how well the shop was initially received. She was up against the specter of the previous shop and its far-from-liked owner.

"I *can't*," Catherine insisted, trying to shrug him off. To her surprise, he didn't remove his hands but kept them—and her—right where they were.

"Slow down," he repeated a bit more firmly. "Otherwise you'll wear yourself completely out before you officially open your doors to the paying public. Then all this work will be for nothing." His eyes held hers, all but hypnotizing her. "Breathe, Catherine, breathe," he instructed.

When she finally did as he instructed, taking a breath in then slowly exhaling it, she never took her eyes off him.

Cody knew defiance when he saw it.

The smallest hint of a smile curved his lips. "That's it, in and out. Good." He slipped his hands from her shoulders, but his eyes continued to hold her in place. "The shop doesn't have to be perfect, you know. *Nothing's* perfect," he underscored.

"I don't want it to be perfect," Catherine protested.

She gestured around the shop helplessly. "I just want it to be…"

"Perfect," he supplied knowingly. "People don't like perfect, Catherine," he told her. "It makes them feel even more imperfect than they already are."

Catherine looked at him for a long moment, clearly surprised. And amused. "I had no idea you were a philosopher, Cody," she said. Maybe she should have called the shop The Philosophical Cowboy, she mused.

Cody inclined his head, amused at her assessment. *You don't know the half of it, Cate.*

"Hell," he said out loud. "I'm a lot of things when I have to be."

Only after a beat had passed did she decide that Cody was just pulling her leg.

Or was he?

Now that she thought of it, a little homespun philosophy actually seemed to be right up his alley.

"How about if I just shoot for clean and presentable?" she suggested, waiting to see what he'd say.

Cody nodded, then qualified his response. "As long as you don't wear yourself out. Okay, I'm finished with this," he said, indicating the large, dapple gray horse that had once been attached to a carousel. Working on it had brought back memories, but none that stopped him in his tracks. He supposed that meant he was making progress. "What's next?" he asked gamely.

"Next," C.C. announced, walking into the shop with a bag that had a wonderful aroma emanating from it, "you stop what you're doing and eat your lunch." Nodding a greeting at Cody, C.C. held the bag she'd brought up to her sister. "You'll find a little of everything in there including a hot pastrami sandwich that tantalizingly announces itself way before you even open the bag and look inside," C.C. cheerfully continued, her sweeping glance taking in both her older sister and the cowboy who had become more or less a fixture in the shop for the last few days.

Catherine frowned. She really didn't have the time to stop and eat right now. "You make this hard to ignore, C.C.."

Her sister smiled broadly. "That, dear sister, is the whole point." She addressed her next words to Cody, issuing a command brightly. "If she doesn't stop to eat, sit on her."

"Will do," Cody promised.

Her errand of mercy over, C.C. left the shop, convinced that Cody would look out for her sister. Cody looked at Catherine expectantly. "You heard the lady."

She had no intention of being ordered around—or intimidated—by her younger sister. "That's not a lady, that's my sister. My *younger* sister," she emphasized as if that made her argument for her.

Cody shrugged. "Younger or older, doesn't matter. What does matter was that she was making sense." Opening the brown bag, he took out the aromatic sandwich and unwrapped the first third. "You need to eat to keep your strength up."

"My strength is just fine," she informed him crisply, determined to ignore both him and the sandwich he was brandishing as she turned her attention to yet another item she'd added to the shop's inventory. This was an extremely fancy saddle that was said to have once belonged to Teddy Roosevelt back in his Rough Rider days, years before he became the country's president.

Not to be put off, Cody warned her, "I'll feed you if I have to."

Armed with the partially unwrapped sandwich, he took a step forward, then another, forcing Catherine to take the same amount of steps backward. Before she knew it, Cody had backed her up against the wall and was using his long, lean body to bracket her in place.

Suddenly, she had no room to move. "Cody, what are you doing?" she protested.

"You must have been without food even longer than I thought if you can't figure it out." Then, in case she was unclear on his intent, he told her, "I'm feeding you for your own good."

She refused to be bullied by either her sister *or* him. "No, you're n—"

The rest of her protest went unsaid because she suddenly found herself confronted with the sandwich that C.C. had left with Cody. Not just confronted with it but her lips were now smack-dab up against it with no leeway to move to the left or to the right. Catherine had no choice but to take a bite or be faced with eventual death by sandwich.

Grudgingly, she chose life.

"There now, that wasn't so hard, now was it?" Cody asked, using the same tone he might have taken with a particularly stubborn five-year-old.

Holding up her hands in the universal sign of surrender, Catherine managed to get a temporary reprieve from her meal.

"Okay, okay," she cried. "I'll eat the sandwich. You can stop force-feeding me. You know, I didn't take you for the nurturing type," she said. There was a slight accusing note evident in her voice.

An enigmatic smile creased his lips. "Like I said, you'd be surprised. I'm not the one-dimensional cowboy you seem to think I am," Cody told her.

Although, in her defense, he added silently, he'd been coming across that way for a while now. Eight years to be exact. But all that was behind him. Right now, he felt as if he'd just woken up from a long, long sleep. Just like the fictional Rip Van Winkle. Woke up to a whole new world around him. Woke up with a desire to *explore* that new world.

"I never thought you were one-dimensional," she protested, then added, "just maybe not all that articulate. But if I insulted you, I'm sorry." That had never even crossed her mind. The last thing she wanted was to make him feel belittled by her.

Cody inclined his head. "Apology accepted," he said mildly. Then he pointed out, "You've stopped eating."

"Only for a second," she quickly countered. "I was taught never to talk with my mouth full."

There was a simple solution to that. "Then don't talk, eat. I'll work, you chew," he told her, assigning a new, albeit temporary division of labor. "That should work for you."

What worked for her, Catherine realized with a silent mental jolt, was Cody. Having him around made her blood rush a little faster, her heart beat a little harder. It energized her and, she had to admit, really scared her at the same time.

She'd told herself that it was this venture that scared her, that made her act as nervous as a cat on a hot tin roof, but she was beginning to realize that her nerves concerning opening the store were actually hiding the bigger, real cause for her internal unrest. She'd found herself in uncharted territory. What was unfolding between Cody and her was something she had never experienced before, especially not to this degree of intensity.

She wanted him.

Badly.

And that both excited her and frightened her to the very brink of near paralysis.

But this was no time to suddenly become immobile. There was much too much to do. She couldn't allow herself the luxury of wallowing in her feelings and thinking rather than doing.

"You're not chewing," Cody noted, his serious tone prodding her on. "I can always take over feeding you again."

Even that had her blood heating. Which in turn sent a pink hue to her face she neither wanted nor liked. Embarrassed, she snapped, "I'm eating, I'm eating."

Cody nodded his approval, managing to get under her skin yet again. "Atta girl," he said, turning his attention back to work.

She mumbled something unintelligible in response. He didn't ask her to repeat it. He had a feeling it was better that way all around.

She'd both dreaded and anticipated this moment. And now, here it was. The moment when she threw open her doors, officially declaring the shop, Real Vintage Cowboy, to be open for business.

The second she opened the doors, the people who had been waiting outside like groupies at a rock concert gate poured in.

Granted the first wave had only ten people in total, but the second those people crossed the threshold, they instantly transformed into ten customers, customers looking to buy something unique to take home with them.

Catherine had gone to great lengths to keep prices on the low side, allowing more people to be able to make purchases. Going this route, it would take her a while to finally turn a profit and get ahead, but if the prices started out being prohibitively high, then she would never be able to get the shop out of the red and finally into the black. And that, after all was said and done, was her ultimate goal.

In next to no time at all, it began to feel as if she was everywhere at once, talking to one group of people, directing another to the food that she'd been up all night preparing, exchanging more words with yet another cluster of friends, family and curious strangers.

Catherine knew she was running on pure adrenaline and at least for now, she was going strong. And each time she rung up a sale, she felt as if she was becoming a little stronger.

It was going very, very well.

Midway through the evening, Catherine forced herself to stand back and take the entire scene in. Her shop was crowded with well-wishers who were doing double duty as the shop's customers as well. She was pleased to note that she had sold more than a token number of items, including the armoire that she'd thought no one would be interested in buying.

At this point, she'd sold enough to make her believe that she had made the right decision when she'd bought the old antique store. Impressed with what he saw of her inventory, her cousin Grant, who managed the Thunder Canyon Resort, had promised to feature some of her merchandise in the hotel gift shop.

It was all starting to fall into place, Catherine thought, pleased and, more than that, greatly relieved.

It seemed that everyone she had ever known had made the effort and shown up at the shop's grand opening. They were now all milling about, examining everything from trendy knickknacks to the paintings she'd hung up on the wall to the original antique furniture that had, along with the shop, passed into her hands when she'd paid the asking price.

Someone, she'd noted with no small pleasure, had actually bought the old-fashioned sewing machine she'd pulled out of the storage room. She'd worked hard to polish the faded black metal until it all but gleamed seductively at one and all who passed by.

And now it had a new home. She felt rather proud of that. She hoped that the machine's new owner would treat it with patience and love. And remember that it worked strictly by man power. That meant pumping the foot pedal rhythmically in order to get the machine to sew. In effect it was almost a unilateral tap dance.

It turned out that the buyer's great-great-grandmother had been a seamstress in a factory from the age of fourteen until her eyesight failed her at seventy. The woman was long gone, but the man had bought the machine to remind him of his roots.

Each piece Catherine sold had a story to tell. But in this case, the story had belonged to the buyer, not the item that was sold.

She loved this, Catherine thought, looking around the showroom. Absolutely loved this.

"Hard to believe that this place never saw any foot

traffic when old Jasper Fowler owned it," she heard DJ Traub say to someone.

Both DJ and Dax had brought their wives to the opening. Dax's wife had already bought two items and gave no sign of stopping there.

"He wasn't trying to make a go of it, he was too busy laundering money for that no-good thief Arthur Swinton," Dax chimed in.

As far as Dax was concerned, he and his brother had an extra reason to despise the old man. "Hey, you remember when Swinton went around claiming that he'd kept company for a time with Mom?" DJ asked his brother.

"Remember?" Dax echoed. "Hell, I had to restrain myself from teaching that old liar a lesson whenever I saw him."

"He wasn't a liar," Forrest Traub interjected. "At least, not about keeping company with your mother."

The look in DJ's eyes hinted that if anyone except for his cousin had just said that, he would have found himself communing with the floor and sporting a black eye. "You've had too much punch, cousin."

"No, no, he's right," Braden, Forrest's brother, chimed in. "It's kind of foggy now," he admitted, "but I seem to remember that Swinton *did* go out with your mother and it was more than once. It was for a while."

The outrage, mingled with horror, that Dax experienced at the mere *thought* of his mother seeing a low-life like Arthur Swinton was all but overwhelming. For a second, it looked as if he was going to throttle his cousin. But his wife intervened by hooking her arm through his and pulling Dax over toward one of the paintings exhibited on the back wall while Allaire did the same with DJ, saying she wanted him to look at some unique bookends she was thinking of buying.

The two women managed effectively to bring an end to the heated discussion.

But not an end to the haunting possibility that there was some truth in the story that the ex-mayor had told after all.

Catherine breathed a sigh of relief. For a moment there, she'd thought that she was going to have to act as a referee and break up a fight between DJ, Dax and their Rust Creek cousins, Forrest and Braden. Although, she had to admit, she was sympathetic to DJ and his brother. True or not, she wouldn't have wanted stories about her mother dating Swinton to be making the rounds.

Turning away from the remaining Traubs, Catherine almost bumped right into Cody.

"Sorry," she murmured, taking a step back.

She'd had no idea that he'd been so close, although she should have sensed it, she told herself. Lately she had developed this sixth sense when it came to the cowboy. Whenever he was nearby, she could feel the hairs on the back of her neck standing up as if they were acting on an attraction all their own.

Rather than say anything in response, Cody wordlessly took her by the hand and led her toward the back of the shop. Puzzled, assuming he wanted to show her something, Catherine allowed herself to be led off.

But instead of showing her something inside the shop, he opened the back door and took her outside.

Stunned, Catherine tried to pull her hand away. When he kept on holding it, it just increased her confusion. "Cody, let go of my hand. I can't just walk out like this. I've still got a shop full of customers in there."

"Relax, they're not going anywhere," he assured her. "They're too busy talking, looking and scarfing up all that food you put out. Take a couple of minutes," he coaxed. "Beautiful though you are, nobody's going to miss you if you're gone for just a couple of minutes or so."

All she really heard was that he'd called her beautiful.

Chapter Eleven

It took Catherine a couple of minutes to finally find her tongue.

"You think I'm beautiful?" she asked. Each syllable echoed with disbelief.

She was serious, he realized.

Cody looked at her quizzically. There were several ornate mirrors hanging in her shop. Didn't she ever look into any of them?

"Well yeah, sure. Don't you?"

She'd always been the dependable one, the den mother who was always looking out for and making things easier for her siblings. She was the one who both her parents turned to whenever they'd needed a responsible person to handle something. No one had ever really commented on her looks. At various times and occasions, her sisters were complimented on their looks, but she was always the one with "the level head on her shoulders."

Shaking her head now, Catherine laughed dismissively. "Not even close."

"Then I'd go see about getting a pair of glasses first chance I got if I were you. Because you are," he told her in a matter-of-fact, no-nonsense voice that testified he was neither trying to flatter her nor gain her favor unfairly. A half smile played on his lips as he looked at her. "Pink's not exactly my favorite color," he told her, "but it works on you."

Where had that come from? She was wearing a royal blue dress, not a pink one. "Pink?" she questioned, looking down at her dress.

Touching her as lightly as possible, Cody ran his callused fingertips along one of her cheeks. "Pink," he repeated.

And then it came to her.

Oh, God, she was blushing again.

Embarrassed, Catherine turned back toward the door and murmured, "I really have to go back inside."

But, unwilling to release her so quickly, Cody didn't let go of her hand.

"And you will," he told her patiently. "I just want you to take a minute to appreciate what you've just accomplished."

She wasn't sure exactly what he was referring to. "And just what have I accomplished?" she asked him.

"You brought that old store full of flea-bitten stuff nobody wanted back from the dead, that's what you've accomplished. Not everyone could have pulled it off, made people look at this decrepit old place in a new light. Make them forget that it was once owned by that crazy old man Fowler," he emphasized.

She thought of the look on DJ's face when his cousin mentioned Fowler's partner in crime, the ex-mayor of their town, hinting that there actually *had* been something between their mother and Mayor Swinton.

"Not everyone is so ready to forget," she interjected.

"Most," he amended obligingly. "And from what I saw, you did some handy business tonight." He saw that she was shrugging this off as well. Didn't the woman know how to take a compliment? he wondered. Especially since she'd earned it? "All I'm saying is take a minute, savor it. Take a deep breath of this pure Montana air, look up at the stars," he pointed out, then said, "Take a minute just to *be*." Ever so slowly, he drew closer to her. Close enough to feel her breath along his skin. "You're rushing around so much, Cate, you're not taking the time to enjoy what's happening. None of it's worth it if you don't take the time to enjoy it," he told her quietly.

She was acutely aware of Cody's closeness. When had he put his arm around her shoulders? She didn't remember him doing that, yet there it was, lightly resting on her shoulders, drawing her into him just as much as the sound of his voice did.

"Okay," she allowed quietly, trying to still the erratic beat of her pulse, "I'm taking a breath, I'm looking up at the stars." She did each as she spoke, then, enveloped in an almost unbearable warmth, she looked up at him. "Now what?" she wanted to know, her question a barely audible whisper.

He was going to say, "Now do it again." But somehow, the words were shanghaied before they ever had a chance to emerge, evaporating into the night air as he found himself bending his head and brushing his lips against hers. Softly, lightly, and then again with just a little more intensity.

Even so, that same wondrous feeling exploded in his veins, that feeling that fairly shouted of his longing for her.

This wasn't the time or the place to act on any of his urges, and he had to pull back now, before his logic just burned away to a crisp in the ever-growing heat of his desire for this woman.

Catherine was surprised that she was still standing, given the fact that her knees had just melted away to nothing. When Cody drew back, she'd been leaning into him, her body speaking to his in a timeless language that needed no words. It took her another second or so to realize that her eyes were closed. Forcing them open, she sternly ordered herself to suck it up and pull herself together, but she knew she was still trembling when he looked at her.

"What are you afraid of, Catherine?" he asked, gently pushing her hair away from her face.

Catherine tossed her head and said with far more bravado than she was feeling, "That my customers will go away if they can't find someone to ring up their purchases."

Not knowing how much longer she could hold her ground—Cody seemed to have the ability to see right through her—Catherine quickly turned on her heel and all but ran back inside.

"No," Cody said to the empty evening air, "that's not it."

Cody remained where he was for a few minutes, allowing Catherine to have her space. When he finally did go back inside, he saw her in the midst of a crowd of her friends, laughing, flitting from one person to another, playing the role of the friendly neighborhood shop owner to the hilt.

The word "playing" stuck in his head for the remainder of the evening.

He decided to stay out of her way, merely observing her as she continued interacting with the people who had come to either be supportive of her or to satisfy their curiosity about the reincarnated shop.

For her part, Catherine made no effort to seek him out, no effort to even say anything at all to him. If he were assessing the situation honestly, he would have had to say that she was going out of her way in order to avoid him.

For the time being, he decided to let things remain that way. He'd obviously shaken her up and until they both understood why, it might be best for both of them if they stayed apart for a while. It wasn't in his nature to push.

But you did this time, didn't you? a voice inside his head taunted.

Maybe he *had* come on a little too strongly, Cody silently conceded, but that had come as a surprise to him as well. God knew he never expected to feel *anything* again, let alone the degree of attraction that he felt taking hold whenever he was anywhere around Catherine.

It was that first spur-of-the-moment kiss that had triggered it, he thought.

Ever since then, he'd found himself seeing the world differently. Seeing *her* differently. And his own part in his life had taken center stage again. He wasn't sleep-walking through life anymore, wasn't just standing on the sidelines the way he had these last eight years. And while he was still working through some residual guilt over being able to finally move on, it really *did* feel good to be alive again.

He just had to convince Catherine that she wanted the same thing he did: a relationship that, as it grew in intensity and scope, would eventually culminate in marriage.

Perhaps even sooner than later.

Life was good.

The amount of business she'd done that first day hadn't just been a fluke or flash in the pan. A week after the shop's grand opening and customers were still turning up, still buying. Not out of acts of kindness or blind support but because they *liked* what they saw.

She knew she owed that, at least in part, to Cody. In tapping into the cowboy's preferences, she'd managed to unearth the kind of things that held genuine appeal for the average citizen of Thunder Canyon. She'd never been so wildly busy or felt so happy and fulfilled, so empowered before.

Or so scared, either, she silently admitted in a rare moment of respite from the steady traffic of questing customers. Scared because the feelings she had whenever she thought of Cody—and she thought of Cody *all* the time—were so incredibly strong she felt that they could very easily overpower her.

Since that first day, he was never far from her thoughts.

Hell, he was in them *all* the time. While she was talking to customers, opening the shop up in the morning, closing the shop down at night, Cody's face would suddenly rise up in her mind without warning, his voice echoing in her head.

Making her lose her train of thought.

She had to work extra hard to keep her growing clientele from thinking she'd lost her mind.

Maybe she actually *had* lost her mind, Catherine thought. How else did she explain the overwhelmingly strong feelings she was having about a man she'd know for less than a month?

This wasn't the reaction of a woman viewed by one and all as "the level-headed one."

It just didn't make sense.

And yet, there it was, part of her every waking moment and part of her dreams as well.

Maybe if Cody continued to stay away, as he had these last few days, she had a chance—albeit a slim one—of getting over him, of actually getting back to the way her life had been before a racing pulse had become her normal state of existence.

Why *hadn't* she seen Cody these last few days? she wondered uneasily. Had he felt rebuffed that night at her grand opening when she'd hurried back inside, leaving him just standing there? Had she wounded his pride because she'd chosen the store over him?

And if she had wounded his pride, how did she undo that?

Catherine pressed her lips together. All she was doing was succeeding in making herself crazy, she silently admonished.

When she heard the tiny bell ring, announcing yet another customer, she was relieved by the diversion.

Pasting a wide smile on her lips, she turned around to greet whoever it was.

"Hello, welcome to the Real Vintage— You," she cried abruptly.

"The real vintage me?" Cody pretended to roll the words she'd just uttered over in his head, frowning as if he was trying to make sense of the greeting.

"Cowboy," she said, supplying the last part of the shop's name. "Cowboy," she repeated with emphasis through clenched teeth. He knew damn well what she'd meant to say, she thought, exasperated. "Where've you been?" she asked before she could think to stop herself.

The smile on his lips was equal parts mystery and satisfaction.

"Miss me?" he asked innocently.

Underneath it all he was relieved because until just this moment, it had all been a gamble for him. He'd been dealing with the very real possibility that she might not have missed him at all. But one look at her face told him that she apparently had. All was well with the universe.

"Yes. No," Catherine quickly amended, not wanting to appear too eager. But then she shrugged, knowing that to pretend that she hadn't missed him was tantamount to telling a lie.

So, in order to save face, Catherine compromised and settled on "Kind of." She waited a beat, then asked again, "So, where were you?"

"I had some catching up to do on the ranch." Which was true, although Hank and Kurt were more than capable of running the ranch and training the horses for a few days at a time. "Besides, I figured I'd let you get being exclusively a shop owner out of your system."

She raised her eyebrows. Now what was *that* supposed to mean? "Oh, you did, did you?"

"Yup." His grin was completely unassuming and incredibly boyish, despite his age. "Also figured that after five whole days of that, you might be ready for a break, so here I am. Consider me as your break."

Her eyes narrowed and she tried very hard to look indignant. After all, he couldn't just waltz in here after five days of hibernation and think he could just take over this way.

Oh, who was she kidding? This wasn't the time to mark her territory. She was just happy to see him. Exceedingly happy. "What did you have in mind?" she wanted to know.

That was when Cody held up the large wicker basket he'd brought in with him. "Guess."

She couldn't just jump into his arms after he'd deliberately stayed away. It would be setting some kind of precedent. Moreover, it would be giving him permission to take her for granted, letting him know that she'd always be waiting for him to make his appearance no matter how long he stayed away.

She was her own person, damn it. That meant that she couldn't have him thinking that he could just pop up after pulling a disappearing act and all would be summarily forgiven.

"Look," she began, doing her best to sound annoyed, "you might think you know me, that you can read me, but you don't and you can't."

"Is that so?" he asked, setting the basket down on the counter.

Summoning her bravado, Catherine raised her chin

as she tossed her head. Silken brown hair went flying over her shoulder. "Yes, that's so."

The words sounded angry. But inside, she was trembling, praying that she hadn't overplayed her hand.

Damn it, he had her so twisted up inside she didn't know what to feel, how to react.

What to want.

"Damn, but you are stirring me up like a pot of stew over a campfire flame when you do that," Cody told her.

She wasn't aware of doing anything out of the ordinary. "Do what?"

Catherine barely got the words out before her lips were rendered immobile. Or rather, recruited for another activity that did *not* involve talking.

She wanted to protest, to cling to her shredded indignation and tell Cody that he wasn't following the rules, wasn't behaving the way she thought he should.

But it was very, very hard to be indignant when her whole body felt as if it was on fire even as it was radiating insurmountable joy.

One kiss from this cowboy and her thought process was reduced to a pile of useless rubble.

What was worse was that she didn't care.

Giving herself permission to enjoy this one kiss, Catherine wrapped her arms around her rough-hewed cowboy's neck. In response, Cody swept her into his arms and her feet lost contact with the ground—just as the rest of her lost contact with the world around her and slipped effortlessly into the one he was creating just for the two of them.

You'd think, she tried in vain to reason, that she would be getting used to his kisses by now instead of lighting up like a Christmas tree inside each and every time his lips found hers.

It wasn't getting old; it was getting better. And better.

As she sighed in utter wonder and contentment, Cody gently set her back down. And then he stepped back, away from her. Taking a second to pull himself together, Cody took her hand and led her to the front door before she realized what was happening. With the picnic basket handle slung over his forearm, he flipped the open for business sign that hung in her window over so that it now proclaimed: Closed. Please come back tomorrow.

He was closing down her store. He couldn't do that, she thought in sudden agitation.

"But it's the middle of the day," Catherine protested. Wanting to sound angry, she realized that her voice sounded oddly compliant to her.

"Yeah, I know," Cody acknowledged. "Best time to have a picnic," he added with a wink.

Once outside, he waited for her to lock the door, then he took her over to where his truck was parked.

"Where are we going?" she asked uncertainly as she got into the passenger side.

"To my ranch," he answered, turning on the ignition. He backed out of the parking space slowly, then pressed down on the accelerator once he was in Drive. "There's someone I want you to meet."

She couldn't begin to imagine who he was referring to. Had his sister come for a visit?

"Who?" Catherine asked, unable to contain her curiosity.

"My horse."

"Your horse?" she echoed incredulously. "You want me to 'meet' your horse?" Was that some kind of code? Or a joke? Cody couldn't possibly be talking about an actual horse—could he?

"Uh-huh." He looked at her as they stopped at one of the few lights in Thunder Canyon. The bewildered look on her face made him laugh. "Honey, you can't begin to understand a 'real vintage cowboy' if you haven't met his horse."

His laugh, deep and rich, wrapped itself around her, instantly heating her blood. Catherine settled back in her seat. "Can't wait," she told him.

He knew she was being flippant, but she was coming along—in more ways than one—and that was all that really mattered to him.

Chapter Twelve

They'd been driving to his ranch for several minutes when he turned to Catherine and asked, "Can you ride?"

"In a car," she answered, her expression the personification of innocence.

"No, a horse," Cody corrected. "Have you ever ridden a horse before?"

He knew that just because this was Montana didn't automatically mean that everyone listed horseback riding as being among their skills. Some people were even afraid of horses.

It hadn't occurred to him until just now that Catherine might be in that group. Mentally crossing his fingers, he really hoped that wasn't the case.

"Does sitting on a pony and having my picture taken at the age of five count?" she asked him, obviously amused by his question.

He made a right at a large oak tree and kept driving. His ranch house was now visible in the distance. "That all depends," he allowed.

She wasn't exactly sure what Cody meant by that. "On what?"

Even if she'd never ridden a horse, as long as she was game to try, that was all that counted. "On whether the photo was taken at a full gallop or not."

"Not," she answered. "Neither the pony nor I were galloping at the time," she assured him. She added, "It was a very docile pony."

So posing for a picture atop the pony hadn't spooked her. That led him to a logical question. "If that was the case, why is it that you never went horseback riding after that?"

She lifted her slender shoulders in a careless shrug as she continued looking around and taking in the scenery. There was a sprawling ranch house in the distance that looked at if it could have accommodated three families, not just one lone man.

Didn't he get lonely rattling around that big old house by himself?

"Too busy with everything else to take the time I guess," she told him. "Is that your ranch house?" she finally asked, unable to bank down her curiosity any longer.

He nodded. "That's my ranch house," he acknowledged, sounding about as cheerful as she'd ever heard him. "Stables are to your left." He pointed them out to her.

Coming to a stop before the house, he parked and got out. Going around the vehicle, he came over to the passenger side. He held the door open for her. Once she was out, Cody leaned in to retrieve the picnic basket from the backseat.

"Almost forgot this." His laugh was self-mocking. Hooking his arm through hers, Cody ushered her toward the aforementioned stables. "I picked out a really gentle horse for you, just in case." He didn't want to give her a headstrong animal that insisted on getting its own way, not if she was unfamiliar with how to handle a horse. Besides, getting a spirited horse might give her an excuse not to ride with him. "Looks like I was right." His smile was encouraging, coaxing. "C'mon, let's go meet your horse."

An uncertainty nibbled away at her, an uncertainty that had nothing to do with the proposed riding session. Cody was moving fast, maybe too fast.

If something moved forward fast, it could also move on just as fast, she reasoned, leaving her behind in the dust. She wasn't sure if she wanted to risk that. Wasn't sure if being with Cody for only a little while was something she could accept.

"My horse?" she echoed quizzically.

"Well, your horse for the day," Cody qualified. "You can't go riding without a horse."

Okay, she'd play along, Catherine thought. "And why am I going riding?"

"Because the perfect place for a picnic is at the top of a bluff. The view you get there is guaranteed to take your breath away," he promised.

"Do I really want to be breathless on a picnic?"

It took him a moment to realize she was pulling his leg. He grinned. "You do this time."

Catherine nodded, accepting his answer. But she

still had another question for him. "And you can't get there by truck?"

"Nope."

Okay, he silently admitted, he was stretching the truth a bit. In reality they actually *could* access the bluff that way, but it was a mite tricky. One wrong move and they could find themselves sliding back down the incline. Getting there by horse was a lot safer and, as far as he was concerned, a lot more pleasurable.

Cody set the basket down right behind the stable door. The last thing he wanted was to have one of the horses come over to investigate the tempting aroma emanating from the basket. Most likely it would be knocked over on its side and scavenged, a casualty to the animal's curiosity.

Cody placed his hand on the small of Catherine's back and gently prodded her into the stable.

He brought her over to the first stall. "This is Buttercup," he told her, introducing her to a mare the color of light butterscotch. The horse had a small white star on its forehead that almost matched the color of her mane. "She's very gentle," he promised Catherine. Then, turning to the mare, he said, "Buttercup, this is Catherine. Go easy on her—she's new at this. Be sure not to spook her."

Catherine didn't know whether to be amused or worried. "You talk to your horses?"

He looked surprised that she would even ask. "Why not? They understand me about as well as people do. Sometimes better," he amended. "Pet her muzzle," he coaxed. Then he said to Catherine with a grin, "I'm talking to you, not the horse, in case that wasn't clear."

This time, she was amused. Hesitating at first, she

gently ran her hand along the horse's sleek muzzle. Buttercup remained perfectly still, as if she understood that she couldn't make any sudden moves.

Catherine smiled as she continued stroking the mare. "She's a beauty," Catherine enthused.

"Funny," Cody told her thoughtfully, "that's exactly what she was thinking about you."

Catherine looked at him sharply. "You can't know what a horse is thinking," she protested.

Cody's mouth curved, a completely unfathomable expression on his face. His tone gave nothing away, either. "You'd be surprised."

Hank walked into the stable in time to hear the last exchange between his boss and the attractive guest he'd brought.

"I wouldn't put nothin' past this man if I were you, ma'am," he warned amiably. "I've seen him tame and charm a horse that was behavin' as if he had the devil himself inside of him. Nobody could handle Wildfire but this here boss man," the man testified with a solemnity that rang with pride.

And then the tall, wiry man touched two fingers to the brim of his worn, weather-beaten hat as a sign of respect and said, "My name's Hank, ma'am, and I've been working for the boss man here for close to five years now—in case he didn't mention me," he added by way of an explanation for his talkativeness. The lines on his weathered face deepened as he smiled slyly and looked at Cody. "I can see why you've been going into town so much lately. She's a real looker."

Out of the corner of his eye, Cody could see color begin to creep up Catherine's cheek. Hank's comment had embarrassed her.

"Since you seem to have so much time on your hands, McCarthy, why don't you saddle Buttercup for the lady?" It was more of an order than a request.

Aware that he might have unintentionally crossed over a line, the ranch hand snapped to attention.

"Oh, yeah, sure thing, boss man." But despite his hurry to do as Cody instructed, Hank paused for one extra minute, smiling directly at Catherine. "Really nice meeting you, ma'am." And, after a quick tip of his hat, the ranch hand went to fetch a saddle for the mare.

"Don't pay any attention to Hank," Cody told her, feeling the need to explain the man's actions. "He's not used to having anyone come to the ranch."

She looked at Cody to see if he was teasing her. But his expression looked serious. "You don't have any visitors at all?"

He shook his head. There was a time when the ranch rang of laughter and the sound of company coming and going. But that had all ended when Renee left his life. Now it was only about getting the job done. For eight years, that had been his only focus.

Until now.

"Visitors get in the way of the work," he told her bluntly.

She couldn't imagine what being isolated on a ranch like that was like. As far back as she could remember, there were always people around her. Granted at times it was just the family, but when there are seven other siblings as well as two parents, "just" the family could amount to quite a crowd.

Apparently his life was the complete opposite of hers, Catherine thought. "Doesn't that get lonely?" she wanted to know.

He looked at her for a long moment. What was he looking for? she wondered. What did he see? "It didn't before."

The way he said it made her think that perhaps Cody had reassessed his lifestyle recently and found it to be lacking. Was it that the loneliness had finally penetrated so deeply that he had become dissatisfied with his lot and decided to see about changing it or was she just reading too much into his tone, turning it into what she *wanted* to hear? She honestly didn't know. All she knew was that she didn't want him to be lonely anymore. She wanted him to be happy.

Within the quarter hour, their horses saddled and ready, they were about to head toward the bluff. The picnic basket Cody had prepared was strapped down and anchored across his saddle horn. Mindful of disturbing it, Cody swung himself into his saddle, carefully avoiding jostling the basket.

As he took his reins into his hands, he glanced at Catherine and promised her, "Don't worry, we'll take it slow."

He was completely unprepared for the gleam he saw suddenly entering her eyes as she listened to what he had to say.

"Slow is for old people!" she declared with a laugh.

The next thing he knew, she kicked her heels into the mare's flanks and cried, "Let's go, Buttercup. Let's show him what you've got."

Before he could say a word or even register his total surprise, Catherine was galloping away, essentially leaving him and the stallion he was riding staring after her, dumbfounded.

He'd been played.

It took Cody less than a heartbeat to come to. The second he did, he pressed his heels into Wildfire's flanks, urging the horse to give chase. The horse obliged at lightning speed.

Cody caught up to Catherine quickly enough, despite the fact that Buttercup'd had a decent lead. Fast as she was, the mare was no match for his own mount, a horse he'd picked for speed as well as his willingness to be trained—once the stallion was finally tamed.

When the two horses were finally side by side, Cody leaned over his own mount and grabbed the reins out of Catherine's hands, pulling her mare—and her—to a dead stop.

The look in Cody's eyes was part surprise, part annoyance. "Why didn't you tell me you could ride like that?" he demanded.

It took her a couple of seconds to stop laughing and answer him. She hadn't meant to trick him, but when he given her an opening, she just couldn't resist playing the part of a helpless novice.

Catherine prefaced her explanation with an apology, hoping that would erase any hard feelings he might be nursing.

"I'm sorry. But you seemed so caught up in your role as the big, protective cowboy, I thought I'd let you enjoy it for a while." She tried to keep a straight face, but it was next to impossible. Laughter kept bubbling up in her throat. "You should have seen your face when I kicked Buttercup's flanks. You looked as if you thought I'd lost my mind."

"That's because I *did* think that," he admitted honestly. Either that or she had a death wish. He'd believed her when she'd initially alluded to not being able to ride at all.

Who knew she was setting him up?

Catherine laughed with pleasure again, then took a deep breath as she tried to get herself under control. It wasn't easy at first, but she finally managed. That was when she finally looked around at her surroundings.

Her breath caught in her throat. "You were right," she said almost humbled. "It *is* beautiful up here. And it definitely is the perfect place for a picnic." She flashed him a wide grin that, unbeknownst to her, came very close to unraveling him. "Thanks for making me come, Cody."

Inclining his head, Cody murmured, "You're welcome," just before he dismounted. Untying the picnic basket, he lifted the handle up over the saddle horn and took it down. "That wild ride couldn't have been good for what's inside," he surmised, lifting the lid to look into the basket.

Just as he'd suspected, everything looked as if it'd had an eggbeater applied to it.

Catherine had already slid off her horse. Holding on to Buttercup's reins, she crossed over to Cody. "I'm sure it's fine," she told him, her eyes smiling up into his.

Having her this close to him in a place that meant so much to him made Cody want to toss the basket aside and just sweep her into his arms. Hell, he could feast on her lips alone for hours.

The temptation was almost overwhelming. But despite the whimsical way she was behaving this afternoon, Cody had a strong gut feeling that if he acted on his impulse, the only thing he'd wind up doing was scaring her off.

There was no doubt in his mind that she was a complex character, this woman who had managed to take his heart out of the deep-freeze it had been residing in these last eight years.

So, with soul-crushing reluctance, Cody reined himself in. Setting the wicker basket down on the ground, he took out the tablecloth he'd packed. With a snap of his wrists, he tried to get the entire tablecloth to gently float down onto the grass in a straight fashion.

The wind had other ideas.

Catching the underside of the tablecloth, the wind wrecked havoc on any hopes of getting the tablecloth down evenly.

Catherine came to his aid, taking two of the corners and pulling the cloth taut.

Between them they spread the checkered tablecloth—how typical, she couldn't help thinking, doing her best not to allow him to see her amusement—out evenly on the grass. Cody quickly placed the basket on one end to anchor down the cloth and then proceeded to empty it out, putting everything he'd packed within Catherine's easy reach.

Within minutes, it was ready.

Catherine sat down cross-legged on the edge of the tablecloth, directly opposite her vintage cowboy. The appreciative look in her eyes was genuine.

"Looks like a feast fit for a king," she told him, then suddenly looked up at him. "Don't tell me you cook, too."

If he had to, he could survive, but there wasn't a hell of a lot of variety in what he could prepare.

"I can make simple things," he admitted freely. "But I didn't make this meal." He had no intentions of taking credit for something he didn't do, even though it might have been fun to see her reaction. "JC did."

"JC?" she repeated. He hadn't mentioned that name to her before. Maybe he wasn't as lonely on the ranch as she'd initially assumed.

"My cook," he clarified, then thought better of his explanation. "Well, he's not really mine. JC used to do the cooking for my mother and father when I first started going to school. When they died, he hung around, making meals for my sister and me even though I told him that I couldn't pay him. He told me not to worry about it, that he was keeping a running tally and I'd pay it off someday. He was only kidding, but I did. I paid him back and when I got the ranch back on its feet again, I officially hired him on."

"And you paid him back every penny you felt you owed him for those years, didn't you?" Cody really didn't have to answer. She knew that he had. She was beginning to know a great deal about this soft-spoken cowboy without actually behind told.

He shrugged as if he couldn't see doing it any other way. "Didn't seem right not to," he told her matter-of-factly.

Catherine could feel her smile spreading when she looked at him. Cody really was a very good man, she couldn't help thinking. Not everyone had as much integrity as he did.

"Someone else would have just chalked it up to having a Good Samaritan intervene. They'd see it as a favor, a good deed done by a man who felt sorry for two motherless orphans. That way, they'd completely forget about paying anything back. But you didn't." She brushed a quick kiss against his cheek, completely surprising him. "You're a very good person, Cody Overton."

The compliment warmed him, but at the same time, it made him uncomfortable. He didn't like being in the spotlight, even for a second. He'd never cared for any undue attention. The truth of the matter was Cody really preferred staying in the background.

Wanting her to focus on something else, Cody nodded at the food he'd spread out.

"Try the fried chicken," he coaxed. "It's JC's specialty. He'd be offended if I came back with any leftovers."

"Well, I wouldn't want to offend the man," she agreed, humor curving her mouth. She picked up a strip of chicken that had been fried to a golden crisp. Biting into it slowly, she was rewarded with an explosion of tantalizing tastes that immediately seduced her. "Wow, this really *is* good," she marveled, more than a little pleasantly surprised.

She'd been prepared to offer lip service about how delicious everything was because, after all, a lot of effort had been placed into this. But she didn't have to fake anything. It really *was* good.

Catherine made short work of the piece she'd been given. Closing her eyes, she savored the taste for a moment. Then, opening them again, she asked, "Does JC share recipes?"

Cody thought before he answered and came up with nothing. "I don't know. I never asked. But I've got a feeling that he would only surrender his recipes on his deathbed—and maybe not even then."

The sound of her delighted laughter seemed to slowly weave its way under his skin and burrow itself deep into his inner core, then it quickly fanned out to effectively take him prisoner.

A willing prisoner.

Cody really wasn't aware of what he was eating. He was only aware of the way Catherine was enjoying herself—and JC's fried chicken.

Aware of that and also aware of the all-too-profound fiery ache he was experiencing in his gut as he watched Catherine squeeze all the enjoyment she could out of the moment.

Chapter Thirteen

"You missed a spot," Cody prompted.

Catherine had surprised him by more than doing justice to the fried chicken he'd packed for their picnic. Wiping her mouth after she'd finished what was her fifth piece of chicken, she'd left behind a tiny crumb at the right corner of her mouth.

Rather than act flustered that she wasn't picture-perfect, the way most of the women he'd gone out with would have reacted, Catherine laughed softly and said, "You're probably thinking that you can't take me anywhere, right?"

She brushed the napkin against her mouth again and somehow still managed to miss the offending crumb.

At a loss for a response, Cody mumbled, "No, I never thought—"

He didn't get a chance to stumble through to the end of his sentence because she asked, "Better?" as she tilted her face beguilingly up for his closer scrutiny.

"No." He nodded at the offending golden speck. "It's still there."

Rather than try again, Catherine surrendered her napkin to him. "Here, you do it. At least you can see what you're doing."

Taking the napkin from her, Cody gently took hold of her chin and with strokes that were even gentler, sent the small, crisp crumb into the grass and parts unknown. He held her chin a second longer, feeling the full impact of the very strong attraction that was radiating between them.

Cody dropped the napkin, leaned closer to Catherine and softly brushed his lips against hers.

There was an instant quickening of his pulse, not to mention his loins, but he didn't want to push anything, didn't want Catherine thinking that he was attempting to take advantage of her in this isolated spot.

Drawing back, Cody looked at her, desperately searching for something to say that wouldn't have him stuttering like some damn fool kid out on his first date—even though that was exactly how she made him feel. As if he was on the brink of something brand-new and exciting that he'd never experienced before.

Wildfire's whinny brought Cody's attention to his mount and, at the same time, to hers. She'd looked like poetry in motion, riding away from him earlier. It had made for a mesmerizing picture.

"Where did you learn to ride like that?" he wanted to know.

There was a fond look in her eyes as she answered, "My Dad put each of us on the back of a horse before we even learned how to walk. He insisted that we all learn how to sit on a horse as if we were part of the animal. He told us that knowing how to ride well could someday save our lives. When you're a kid, you believe everything your father says. I'm sure that watching us learn probably stopped my mother's heart more than once, but in the end, all of us were glad Dad was so adamant about making each of us learn."

Having all but been born in the saddle himself, Cody couldn't argue with that kind of reasoning, but he could definitely take exception with something else.

"You could have given me a heads-up, you know," he told her, "instead of making me look like some damn fool idiot."

Catherine shook her head at the very idea. "I doubt if *anything* could make you look like a 'damn fool idiot.'" The intimacy of the moment gave her the courage to ask something she would have normally pretended to ignore. "Why'd you stop kissing me, Cody?"

The wide shoulders rose and fell swiftly. The question surprised him. "I didn't want you to think I had an ulterior motive, bringing you here."

"So all you wanted to do was just eat?" she asked innocently.

"When you say it like that…" His voice trailed off as he tried to get a handle on whether or not she was serious or putting him on. Did she *want* him to do more than just eat and talk or was she testing him?

His limited experience with women left him at a complete loss for an answer.

"Yes?" Her voice was almost melodic as it coaxed him to continue.

When she looked at him like that, everything inside of him felt as if it had just been thrown into a churning whirlpool—and it was about to go over the side. "Oh, hell, woman, you're driving me crazy."

"Why, Cody?" she whispered, her eyes lowering to his mouth. "Why am I driving you crazy?"

She was less than a heartbeat away from him. He could feel her breath on his mouth when she spoke. His gut tightened.

Instead of saying anything, he showed her. Pulling Catherine into his arms, he kissed her again. Except that this time, there wasn't anything gentle, anything polite about the way his mouth covered hers. This time, there was an urgency to it. Kissing her came across like a matter of survival, that if he *didn't* kiss her just like this, he'd be completely depleted of everything that allowed him to draw breath.

But after a moment, his self-control reared its head again, warning him that a second longer like this and he would have gone over the edge, gone to a place from which there was no turning back, at least not for him.

So with his very last ounce of strength, even though everything within him was screaming for him not to stop, Cody pulled back again.

"*That's* why you're driving me crazy," he almost shouted, his frustration taking solace in unproductive anger.

Rather than scare her off or at least make her back away, creating a safe distance between them the way he'd hoped this display of temper would accomplish, Catherine whispered, "The feeling's mutual," saying the words so close to his lips that they almost seemed to come from him instead.

The words sealed his doom.

"Oh, damn," Cody groaned again, giving up the fight. Taking her and surrendering to her at the same time.

The next moment, Catherine was back in his arms again and his mouth was pressed against hers. Except this time, he knew he wasn't having his way with her. It was mutual. She was having her way with him as much as he with her.

And *that* triggered almost a frenzied response within him, a frenzy that at the same time dictated that he exercise extreme control over himself, otherwise these wild, strange feelings would all wind up crashing into one another, and who knew the consequences of that?

No matter what, Cody wanted some semblance of control over her, over himself so that his struggle, as it happened, wouldn't seem as if it had all been triggered by her. Because *that* would certainly remove the last shred of power from his hands.

But maintaining restraint wasn't easy, not when she moaned the way she was moaning. Not with the way she felt like liquid gold in his hands, hot, pliable and so very spellbinding and enticing.

Though he doubted if she would even understand if he told her, it was restraint that had his hands running along the curves of her body like this. He was employing restraint because he was touching her while leaving her clothes where they were. They served as barriers against his eager palms and questing fingers.

All in good time, a voice in his head whispered.

But before Cody could act on the insistent impulse that was throbbing in his brain, to his stunned surprise, Catherine began opening buttons. *Catherine* was the one removing layers of her clothing, pushing aside material so that he could touch her bare skin.

And when he did, it was his turn to groan. To groan and grow short of breath as the very air seem to heat up between them.

There was no path to satiation.

The more Cody touched her, the more he wanted to touch her.

And the more he wanted her.

His breath all but backed up in his throat when she slipped her hand underneath his shirt, her fingers splayed, then moving as she seemed intent on memorizing the very contours and hard ridges of his chest.

For the life of him, Cody couldn't have said which of them actually unbuttoned his shirt or pulled it from his shoulders and torso, tossing it aside in a bunched-up heap. Or, for that matter, which of them wound up disposing of the rest of Catherine's clothing.

It all occurred within an all-consuming haze, marked by sudden, hot arrows of passion that pierced right through him, reminding him what it meant to want a woman, to make love *to* a woman as well as *with* her.

Catherine became all things to him at once, a revelation, a homecoming and a humbling novelty all rolled up into one.

She had no idea what came over her.

She'd never in her life reacted this way before, never wanted what she wanted at this moment before. The power within Cody's kiss made her want to please him, to be desired by him.

Be possessed by him.

Her body had instantly heated when he'd touched his mouth to hers. Suddenly there were passions and desires erupting within her at an incredibly breathtaking pace. Catherine couldn't think clearly, didn't *want* to think at all, just experience all the wondrous sensations that were currently racing through her body, making it sing in a language she'd never known before.

Never known before, but wanted desperately to learn.

Being with Cody this way fueled an eagerness within her, an eagerness that made her almost rip off his clothes in her desire to touch and be touched. To press her naked skin against his equally bare torso.

It seemed to her that Cody instantly conquered every place his lips touched, branding her. Making her his for all time.

Her neck, her shoulders, her belly, the skin all but burned as his mouth passed over each and every area. She twisted and turned, her body eager to spread the sensation, to share it equally even as those sensations continued to explode all along her body.

When Cody came close to her throat, she seized her opportunity, took hold of his face between her hands and kissed him so hard she thought her soul would crack from the impact.

And still it wasn't enough.

She wanted more, craved more even though she had no idea where this rampaging need was coming from or how it was all going to end.

Heretofore she'd been almost docile and had little to no desire to enter this fiery wonderland she was racing through now.

But then, how could someone miss what they'd never known? The small handful of partners she'd had before had never even had the keys to the back door of this exquisite paradise.

Now, however, she knew that when this was gone, she would severely mourn the loss.

Moving by instincts she'd had no idea she possessed until just now, Catherine did her best to teasingly goad him on, silently entreating Cody not to hold back any longer.

Her body ached for him.

As did her soul.

For his part, Cody knew that he'd come close to self-destructing if he didn't take her now, this second. Rolling over so that she was beneath him, he watched Catherine's eyes as he positioned himself over her. Even in this amped-up state, he was watching her eyes for any telltale sign of fear, of hesitation. For some indication that she'd suddenly changed her mind and wanted him to stop before the ultimate act occurred.

But there were no signs, no silent entreaties.

The exact opposite was true.

His hands braced on either side of her, Cody slowly drove himself into her. Almost at the same time, he covered her mouth with his and pulled her close against him, his arms woven tightly around her, sealing the bargain completely.

Ever so slowly, he began to move, to rock. But right from the very start, the pace instantly increased.

And she matched him.

Echoed each movement, returned each thrust until, evenly matched, they found themselves racing higher and higher along that rarified incline. And then, joined, they leaped off the peak together.

Exhilaration seized Cody.

He was breathing so hard, he didn't know if he could ever successfully catch his breath again.

Ultimately, he decided that didn't matter. Because this one time, he'd been part of something that had been exquisitely perfect.

Gradually, he became aware that her short, staccato breaths were lengthening in breadth and scope, as were his own.

And after a few minutes, Cody found he had enough air in his lungs to enable him to form words. But, to play it safe, he took in a few more breaths before venturing to say something.

Catherine hadn't moved a muscle since they'd plunged off the cliff together—now an eternity ago. She remained tucked against him and he had his arm protectively around her.

Turning toward her now, Cody felt he had to make something crystal clear in case he hadn't before. "I want you to know I didn't plan on this."

He could feel the small, guileless smile as it formed on her lips. Watched it as it entered her eyes, all before she finally said, "I know."

Cody raised himself up on his elbow, wanting to get a better look at her face. The smile notwithstanding, she seemed serious, at least about this.

"You know?"

She nodded. Again her eyes crinkled into a smile. "I could *feel* you struggling with yourself."

He sank back down again, trying to make sense out of everything that had just happened and how he was supposed to deal with it. The goalposts ahead seemed clear to him, but he wasn't so sure how to put what he was feeling, what he wanted her to know, into words so that she knew as well.

He began with something he'd already said, wanting to build on it and go from there.

"I didn't want you to feel I was taking advantage of you." He got no further because he could feel her laughing softly. Was she laughing at him or something he'd said? "What's so funny?"

"Taking advantage of me?" she repeated, then reminded him of a very crucial fact in their coming together, "You didn't exactly have to tie my hands and feet to a tree, you know."

"No," he agreed, "but you might think that I seduced you."

Seduced her?

The fact that she didn't burst out laughing testified that she had developed *huge* restraint herself. Catherine congratulated herself.

And then she smiled to herself again. Cody was incredibly sweet. She'd had no idea he could be this thoughtful, this sensitive about her feelings and reactions. Who knew that beneath all that solemnity beat the heart of a kind man who intentionally put her needs ahead of his own?

"If anything, Cody, I seduced you," she told him with a very straight face. And then her grin popped up as she continued, "You did your best to resist. By the way, a girl could get a complex from that, you know."

"A complex?" he repeated quizzically.

"Sure. I started to wonder what was wrong with me if I had to all but rip your clothes off to get you to finally come around and make love with me."

"I came around way before you got started taking my clothes off," he informed her.

"Oh?" She grinned at him. "Really?"

He couldn't tell from her tone of voice if she was teasing him or actually surprised by what he'd just said. Or if she was saying that she didn't believe him.

All he could do was give her an honest reply. "Yes, 'really.'"

"And exactly what was it about me that made you come around?" she wanted to know, not sure if she believed what he was telling her or not. Cody seemed honest enough, but men were known to lie if it suited them.

"Everything," he answered without any hesitation.

"You know, for a taciturn cowboy," she marveled, "you really do have a way with words when you try." Her eyes began to shine as she added, "But I have to admit that I like the fact that you don't need words to get your point across."

It was his turn to feign innocence even though he knew exactly what she was referring to. "Oh?"

Catherine shifted so that she was looking down at him, her long brown hair moving teasingly along his bare chest.

"Yes, 'oh,'" she repeated, mimicking his tone.

Then, before any more dialogue could be exchanged, she moved seductively along his body, her bare torso singeing his.

And then she kissed him as hard as she could, with every fiber of her being.

And just like that, Cody found himself engaged in another exhilarating, mind-bending marathon—and loving it beyond words.

Chapter Fourteen

It was time, Cody decided.

He'd thought on it long and hard these last few days and made up his mind that it was time. Time to move on. Time to have a talk with Catherine about what was on his mind.

But he needed to take care of something else first.

Looking for just the right words that he wanted to use, he didn't notice Hank walking toward him as he hurried down the front steps. Didn't really notice him at all until Hank all but planted his tall, wiry body in front of him.

Hooking his thumbs through his belt loops, Hank asked with a wide, guileless grin, "Is it my imagination, boss, or is that a spring in your step I've been seeing these last few days?"

The look on the man's face was a cross between a smirk and something that looked like vicarious pleasure. Cody knew that if he allowed himself to get sucked into a conversation with his ranch hand, it would throw his schedule completely off. Hank, given half an opportunity, could talk the ears off a bronze statue. He was a damn hard worker, but he had a bad habit of never using five words if he could use fifty instead.

"Your imagination," Cody said crisply, deliberately moving around the man.

Rather than take the hint, Hank fell into step beside him, staying closer to him than a shadow. "No, no, I think that's a definite spring." Hank pretended to take a second, long look at his boss to convince himself. "Yup, that's what it is, all right. A spring." Hank was definitely smirking now. "It wouldn't have anything to do with that nice young woman you brought up to the ranch last week, now would it?" Before Cody had a chance to say "no," Hank boasted, "I've got a keen eye for these kinds of things."

"It's a shame you don't use that keen eye of yours to focus on getting your job done instead of trying to figure out someone else's business," Cody said. There wasn't even so much as a *hint* of a smile on his face or in his voice.

A lot of men would have backed off. But Hank had worked for him since he'd bought the ranch nearly five years ago and he didn't scare easily.

"I can do both," Hank volunteered, punctuating his statement with another wide grin.

"Ask me, it's about time," Kurt chimed in. The second, younger ranch hand seemed to come out of nowhere. "Hank and me were starting to worry that you weren't never gonna come around."

Stopping, Cody looked from one man to the other.

"Is my personal life all you can find to talk about?" he wanted to know.

"Ain't been all that much to talk about until just now," Hank answered. Thumbs still hooked into his belt loops, he rocked back on his heels. "I'd strike real fast if I were you, boss. That little lady isn't going to be single for long. Not with that face and figure."

"I'm with him," Kurt said, jerking a thumb in Hank's direction.

Cody frowned. He knew they meant well, but he wasn't about to start a precedent by condoning this kind of talk from men who were working for him.

"You two through gossipin' like two little old ladies?" he demanded, looking from one to the other, his expression unreadable. "'Cause if this is what you want to be doing, I can hire two hands to take your place faster than you can say 'mind your business.'"

Hank held his hands up in the universal sign for surrender. "We're just being happy for you, boss. No cause for you to go all ornery on us."

Kurt merely shook his head. "Ask me, I don't think he knows how to be happy without acting like a wounded bear," he said as if Cody wasn't standing within three feet of him.

Hank appeared to mull the assessment over. Both men began to walk away from Cody and toward the stable. "Well, that's a habit he's sure gonna have to change if he wants to go on keeping company with that pretty little shopkeeper. There's only so much scowling a woman like that would be willing to put up with before she just walks away," Hank estimated.

Kurt was quick to agree with him. "Ain't that the truth?"

"If you two are through dissecting my life," Cody called after them, raising his voice to be heard, "there's a little matter of cleaning out the stalls to attend to." Cody was doing his level best to sound annoyed, but at the moment, thinking about the life he pictured ahead of him, it was really becoming difficult to maintain a gruff exterior. Especially when everything felt as if it was all rosy inside of him.

Hank stopped just short of the stall entrance. "You gonna go see her?" he wanted to know.

Cody left that part unanswered. Instead, in case they had to come looking for him for some reason, he told the two ranch hands where he was going to be for the next half hour or so. "I'm going to the cemetery."

Kurt came out of the stable, a pitchfork for mucking out the stalls in his hands. He exchanged looks with Hank.

Hank was the one who spoke first. "Uh-oh, you have a setback, boss?" he asked sympathetically.

"Not that I'm aware of," was all Cody would volunteer. With that, he slid into his truck and drove off, leaving both of the ranch hands staring after him, trying to puzzle out just what was going on.

It was too good to be true and she knew it.

He was too good to be true.

These last few days she'd spent with Cody had been as close to perfect as humanly possible—and it had her worried.

Ever since Cody had whisked her away on that impromptu picnic, he'd been turning up at the shop, saying and doing things that absolutely made her heart sing. Cody Overton had turned out to be everything she had ever wanted in a man.

Which, she was convinced, meant that it was all too good to be true. This was more like a dream than reality and everyone knew you had to wake up from a dream sooner or later.

No dream went on indefinitely—did it?

Dreams didn't, but maybe a man did, she thought hopefully. Maybe what she was seeing was the real Cody—the one who was kind and considerate beneath that rough-hewed exterior.

But, more likely, the real Cody had been temporarily sublimated and this was just an aberration, someone who would fade away all too soon once he tired of being like this.

No two ways about it, Catherine realized that she was waiting for the other shoe to drop. And while she was doing this waiting, she kept looking at the clock on the opposite wall, waiting for Cody—any version of Cody—to come walking in.

Because right now he was late, she thought. Not that Cody actually clocked in, of course, but for the last five days, he'd been turning up bright and early and it was no longer early now—and growing less bright by the moment.

As a matter of fact, it was going on close to noon.

Chewing on her lower lip, Catherine glanced at the phone by the register and wondered if she should try to call Cody.

Would that seem too eager to him? Too needy? She didn't want to come across as some clingy female, but if by any chance there was something wrong, she wanted to know.

Cody would have called if he'd decided not to come, right?

The question echoed in her brain as a dozen reasons—both pro and con—assaulted her. She couldn't come up with anything definite on either side.

Unable to talk herself out of it and growing progressively shorter and shorter on patience, Catherine hurried over to the phone and picked up the receiver.

Just as she did, she heard the bell ring behind her. Swinging around to face the front of the store, she cried, "You're finally here," before she could think to stop herself.

The new chef at the Gallatin Room in the Thunder Canyon Resort, Shane Roarke, was surprised at the nature and tone of the greeting. His eyebrows drew together in obvious confusion.

"I guess I am," he murmured, not quite sure how to respond to the shop owner's strange greeting.

Embarrassed, Catherine flushed slightly. The man probably thought she was crazy.

"I'm sorry," she apologized. "I thought you were someone else."

"I'm sorry I'm not," he said with a smile. Putting his hand out, he introduced himself. "Hi, I'm Shane Roarke."

"Catherine Clifton," she responded, returning his handshake.

"I'm new in town and I just bought a place that doesn't have a stick of furniture in it. Someone at the Thunder Canyon Resort said that you've gotten some good, sturdy pieces for sale at decent prices so I thought I'd come in and look around."

Idiot! Catherine upbraided herself. She'd almost lost

a customer, letting thoughts of Cody crowd her head and push everything else out. This was her livelihood she was jeopardizing, and if she wasn't careful, she'd find herself losing everything. She was going to have to keep her mind on business and everything else was going to have to go on the back burner, including Cody.

Easier said than done and she knew it.

Out loud she said, "Please," as she made a sweeping gesture with her hand, taking in most of the shop. "Look all you want. I'm sure you'll find something here to your liking—and on the outside chance that you don't, let me know what you're looking for and I'll see if I can track it down for you at some estate sale."

In the last couple of months, she'd gotten rather good at that, finding small, out-of-the-way places that had both furniture and vintage clothing that seemed to be all but waiting for her to come and rescue them for her shop.

"Any piece in particular on your mind?" she wanted to know.

Shane shook his head. "To be honest, it's one of those things that I'll know it if I see it."

Catherine nodded. "I know just what you mean." And she did. An item had to appeal to her—to "speak" to her—before she made an offer to buy it. "So I'll get out of your way and let you start looking around," she concluded, giving her new potential customer her most accommodating, friendly smile.

Less than two minutes later, her heart leaped into her throat again when she heard the bell go off for a second time.

Swinging around to look, she found that it wasn't Cody walking into the shop this time around any more than it had been the last time. Instead of the tall cow-boy, a very pregnant-looking Antonia Wright crossed the threshold, moving slowly.

Catherine's disappointment faded as she greeted one of her oldest friends. Despite being seven months along, the single mother-to-be was still going strong, running the only boardinghouse in Thunder Canyon and managing to do it all practically single-handedly.

Stubbornness, Catherine thought, was one of the key things that she and Antonia had in common.

"Antonia, what brings you here?" Catherine asked after she gave the woman a quick hug that required some artful bending on her part.

"Swollen feet," Antonia answered wearily. With one hand protectively on her protruding abdomen, she looked at Catherine. "Tell me, do I have two different shoes on?" she asked.

Amused, Catherine looked down, then shook her head. "No, they're both the same. Why?"

"Because the right one feels a lot tighter than it did just a couple of days ago. I thought maybe I made a mis-take and put on two different shoes." Antonia sighed, her frown deepening. "Oh, God, I can't wait—"

"For the baby to be born?" Catherine asked. By the time the seventh month hit, she knew that some women felt as if they'd been pregnant forever and that they'd never have a waist again.

"Well, that, too," Antonia allowed with a vague nod of her head, "but what I was going to say was that I can't wait to see my feet again." Pausing, the blonde looked around at the items on display. "When I came to your grand opening, I saw this rocking chair that really caught my attention—it had carvings along the back headrest. Roses I think or maybe buttercups. Anyway, it looked perfect and I decided to get myself a present. Do you still have it?" she wanted to know.

The mention of buttercups had her thinking of Cody and the horse he's selected for her. And what came after their picnic.

This isn't focusing on work, she admonished herself silently.

Looking at Antonia, she pasted a smile on her lips and beckoned for the woman to follow her.

"It's right back here," she told Antonia, leading the way. She glanced over her shoulder to see if her friend was following her or had decided to forgo the twists and turns of the small, makeshift aisles and was waiting to have the rocking chair brought to her.

"I'm coming," Antonia reassured her, guessing what was on Catherine's mind. "I don't waddle as fast as I used to."

Antonia was forced to stop short or find herself running right into a tall, handsome stranger who possessed a smile that warmed the room, increasing its temperature by at least two degrees.

Why was it that all the good ones were either taken or choosing to pop up now, when she couldn't do anything about it?

The man nodded at her as their paths crossed. He looked vaguely familiar, and then she remembered where she'd seen him before. He was the new chef the Traubs had brought in to work at their resort.

The next moment, the handsome chef had disappeared behind another row of furnishings.

"So, are you thinking about actually buying this

rocking chair?" Catherine asked as she moved the hand-carved chair to a more accessible place.

Gripping the armrests for support, Antonia lowered herself onto the seat. She was trying it out to determine if the rocking chair was wide enough to comfortably accommodate her. Of late, she felt as if she'd spread out like an overfilled cupcake.

"No, I'm just going to sit here until I deliver," she quipped. She rocked a little and smiled. This would do fine. "Speaking of which—" she looked at her friend "—do you deliver or am I going to have to find a way to bring this to my house?"

Even if she didn't have any delivery system, Catherine wouldn't have left Antonia in a lurch. "Don't worry, I'll have one of my brothers deliver it," she promised.

"Excuse me," Shane interrupted politely, popping up again. "I was just wondering—"

Hoping for another sale, Catherine raised her eyes from her friend and turned her attention toward the good-looking bachelor. "Yes?"

"The previous owner, does he still come in once in a while?" Shane wanted to know.

Why would he be asking about Fowler? No one had liked the man even before he'd suddenly kidnapped one of their own in a desperate attempt to escape the law.

"You mean Jasper Fowler?" Catherine asked just to make sure he was actually asking about the man and not someone else. When Shane nodded, she said, "Lord no, I haven't seen him since before I bought the store."

Mercifully, everything had been handled through the bank and she hadn't had to endure any one-on-one dealings with the horrible little man.

Shane took in the answer, but he wasn't finished yet. What neither of the two women knew was that he was actually approaching the heart of his real question, circling it slowly so as not to give himself away until he was ready to.

"Is it true that Fowler was using the store as a front for some kind of an illegal business that actually involved the mayor as well?" Shane was doing his best to sound only mildly curious, the way a newcomer to a town might as he gathered information about his new town.

"Ex-mayor," Catherine corrected pointedly.

The present mayor of Thunder Canyon was a distant cousin of hers and completely upstanding, unlike the double-dealing Arthur Swinton, who'd landed in prison for his misdeeds, then managed to escape. The money he'd wound up skimming thanks to his position as mayor hadn't been found so far.

"But as far as your question goes, that was the general belief," she acknowledged. "However, if you're looking for details, I'm afraid that I don't have any." He'd aroused her curiosity. Most people who came in asked questions about the origins of the furniture and knickknacks, not about the location of the former owner and his supposed cohort. "Why do you ask?"

Shane raised his shoulders in a vague shrug. "No reason, really. I'm just trying to pick up a little background information on the town since I'm new around here."

He'd asked too many questions, Shane thought, frustrated and annoyed with the situation. God knew he didn't want to arouse anyone's suspicions until he was ready to make his move. He definitely didn't want his secret coming out before people thought well of him.

Flashing a smile at Catherine that was also directed at the woman in the rocking chair, he said, "Thanks for your help. I'm going to take a few measurements at home and then I'll be back," he promised.

Tipping his hat to both women, Shane left the shop.

"I certainly hope he'll be back," Catherine murmured loud enough for Antonia to hear. Turning toward her friend, Catherine couldn't help remarking on the obvious. "Now *that* was one good-looking man."

Antonia shrugged. "He wasn't bad," she agreed.

"Not bad? God but you have high standards." Then, looking at Antonia pointedly, she said, "I think he liked you."

Antonia rolled her eyes. "Oh, puh-lease. The man was probably thinking how relieved he was that I wasn't his problem. Trust me, *no* man notices someone in my condition, except in that light." She shifted slightly in the chair. "Speaking of men, how are things going with Cody?"

In her exuberance, she'd shared her thoughts about Cody with Antonia. In hindsight, that might not have been a good idea. Antonia was a little bitter when it came to the subject of men. "So far, so good. To be honest, almost too good," she confided.

Antonia looked at her, then shook her head. "Oh, I know that starry-eyed look. I saw it in my own mirror about seven months ago," she said, unconsciously placing her hand on her swollen belly. "My advice to you is stay grounded and don't let yourself get carried away. Most men, sad to say, don't live up to their own hype. Honey, I don't want to see you disappointed the way I was." She stopped herself from saying more. There was no point in complaining. What was done, she thought, was done. "Remember, you're the only one you can depend on."

There was more than a trace of bitterness in Antonia's voice, but then, Catherine supposed the woman was entitled to it. After all, the man she'd been in love with had suddenly found a reason to disappear, leaving her single and pregnant, neither condition was one that Antonia had foreseen for herself at this point in her life.

"I like it," Antonia declared, changing the subject and nodding at the rocking chair. Struggling, she began to get up in almost slow motion, using the armrests to push herself to her feet. "Ring it up." Antonia began to rummage through her purse for her wallet.

"I'll be happy to. It's a sturdy chair that'll last you a lifetime," Catherine said, slowing her pace as she accompanied her friend to the register.

"Good," Antonia replied, still looking through her purse. "So I can use it in my old age."

"Sounds like a plan," Catherine laughed.

The moment Antonia left the store, Catherine reached for the phone. After talking to her friend, she needed reinforcement. She needed to hear the sound of Cody's voice. It didn't matter what he actually said— as long as it wasn't to tell her that he'd decided not to see her anymore.

Antonia's state of mind had gotten to her, Catherine thought.

She let the phone ring ten times. When it rang for an eleventh time, she gave up and started to hang up. Just before the receiver met the cradle, she thought she heard a deep voice say, "Hello?"

Snatching the receiver back up to her ear, Catherine cried, "Cody?" then upbraided herself for not attempting to sound at least a little calmer. This was going to scare him away for sure.

"No, this is Hank."

Hank. Trying to associate the name with a face, she came up empty for a second, then remembered the ranch hand Cody had introduced her to last week. "Um, Hank, is Cody around? I'd like to speak to him."

"Sorry, ma'am, he's out."

Had Hank been told to say that or was Cody actually out? Crossing her fingers that it was the latter, Catherine did her best to sound upbeat as she asked, "Would you know where he is?"

"Well, last I heard, he said something about going to the cemetery."

"Thank you."

Catherine hung up and stared at the phone.

The cemetery.

That was where Cody went when he wanted to talk to his wife. He'd told her that the other day.

A sinking feeling began to take hold of her. He'd gone to "talk" to Renee. This didn't sound good.

Trying to tell herself that she was overreacting, Catherine nevertheless hurried to the front of the shop. She flipped the closed sign so that it was visible from the outside and then quickly left the store.

She had to find out what Cody was doing at the cemetery.

Chapter Fifteen

Approaching the cemetery, Catherine slowed her vehicle to a near crawl as she looked around for an inconspicuous place to park. Cemeteries were far from her favorite place to be, even in daylight.

As she looked around, she saw Cody's truck parked not too far from the entrance. So much for wondering if he'd actually come here.

Driving farther on, she finally found a space to leave her car that wasn't visible from where Cody had left his vehicle.

Oh, God, she'd gone from vintage/thrift shop owner to stalker, Catherine silently upbraided herself. There was no other explanation for why she'd just closed up shop and driven straight over here in the middle of the day.

And exactly what was she going to do once she located Cody in the cemetery? She had no claim on him.

They'd only been seeing one another—if that was what
it could actually be called—for a little more than three
weeks. Moreover, they'd only become intimate less
than a week ago.

It was all so whirlwind fast with no commitments,
no promises. Which meant that she and Cody were free
to do whatever they wanted with whomever they chose.

Besides, coming here wasn't like Cody was sneak-
ing around, cheating on her with another woman. After
all, a man couldn't cheat on a girlfriend with his own
wife, she thought ruefully.

His *late* wife, she reminded herself, searching for
something to grasp on to.

She couldn't find it. Renee being dead didn't exactly
matter, did it? Dead and gone, the woman could still
come between them if Cody was still in love with her.

Because if he was, then most likely he'd feel guilty
about what they'd been doing together these last few
days. The way he'd talked about Renee that night at
DJ's Rib Shack told her that to Cody, making love with
her was somehow being unfaithful to Renee's memory.

Catherine could feel her anxiety growing.

Oh, God, she thought, resting her head on the steering wheel, what a mess this had turned out to be. Why
couldn't things just be simple for a change?

She was in love with Cody—and at the same time,
afraid of being in love with him. Afraid of being hurt
by him. And he, well he was here at the cemetery,
wasn't he? That could only mean that he felt he owed
his loyalty to Renee.

Her brother Craig had told her that Cody had been
extremely broken up when his wife died. In the months
that followed, he'd turned into almost a hermit, only

venturing out occasionally. Eventually, that changed a little bit, but not a great deal. None of the women he'd been seen with were ever repeaters—no one saw them in his company more than once. It was as if he was determined to keep moving, to keep ahead of anything that even hinted at becoming permanent.

But he'd seen *her* more than just once, Catherine reminded herself. She had obviously broken whatever rules he'd been adhering to.

Except that maybe now that didn't count anymore—because Cody hadn't shown up today. Hadn't come to her shop the way he had for the last few days. Instead, he'd gone to his wife's grave.

To ask for forgiveness?

A spark of hope entered her heart. Maybe she was wrong, Catherine fervently prayed as she finally got out of her car and walked toward the cemetery entrance. Maybe Cody was here visiting his parents' grave—or someone else's for that matter.

It didn't *have* to be Renee's grave that had brought him here.

Clinging to that and crossing her fingers, Catherine walked through the towering black iron gates and entered the cemetery proper.

Cody removed his Stetson as he took a couple of steps back from his wife's headstone. He'd just laid a large bouquet of carnations—her favorites—on her grave.

"I've got something I need to tell you, Renee," Cody said softly, then smiled ruefully. "But you probably figured that out because of the flowers. You always used to say you knew whenever I'd done something I didn't think you'd like because I brought you flowers." He fidgeted slightly. "Some things don't change, I guess." Cody ran his fingers along the brim of his black hat, searching for the right words so that this could come out coherently. "And then, other things do. And that's why I'm here," he confessed, addressing the headstone. "Because something's changed."

Pausing, he took a deep breath then pushed on. This was not easy for him.

"I know that you told me that you wanted me to move on once you weren't here anymore." It was one of the very last things Renee had said to him as her time grew short. As he remembered, emotion threatened to close his windpipe even after all this time.

"And when you said that, I told you that I couldn't. That it was going to be hard for me just living inside each day that you weren't part of anymore. And it was," he told his wife with feeling. "For a long, long time, it was. But I kept breathing and I kept working—and I kept missing you," he admitted.

He paused again, waiting for the tears that threatened to spill out to retreat. A man was supposed to be able to control his grief better than that, not let it control him.

"I *still* miss you," he told his wife in a low voice. "You need to know that, and to know that I'll always love you. You'll always have a piece of my heart, Renee, a big piece.

"But there's someone else who's come along...." And then he laughed at himself. "But I suspect you already know that. Hell," he reflected, "you know everything I'm about to say, don't you?" He smiled at the headstone, remembering Renee the way she used to be before the cancer left its mark on her. "I know you've been lookin' down, watching me so that means you've already seen her. Her name's Catherine Clifton—you know that, too," he realized the next moment, and a touch of irony echoed in his tone. "She makes me happy, Renee. I never thought that was going to be possible, but it is and she does. And I love her. Not like I loved you," he admitted. "You only fall in love for the first time once. So this is kind of different, but it's love all the same."

Cody cleared his throat, his discomfort surrounding him. But he needed to push on. He needed to say all this to Renee. He owed her that.

Or maybe this was just to close a chapter in his life so that he *could* move on.

"So what I'm doing here today, Renee, is asking for your approval. You see, I'm going to be asking Catherine an important question, one I don't know if she's going to say yes to—but I'm hoping." He saw that he was beginning to leave a mark on the brim of his hat and forced himself to stop fingering it. "But I didn't want to ask her before I told you and asked if it was all right with you.

"I'd be obliged if you could find a way to give me a sign, something that'll tell me you're all right with all this. Doesn't have to be anything big," he added quickly. "No bushes set on fire or stuff like that. As a matter of fact, I'd be relieved if you don't burn anything, but just find a way to give me a sign nonetheless."

He stood there for a moment, looking at the headstone. Waiting. Others might have called him a fool or scoffed at what he was doing, but Cody was completely confident that Renee would find a way to let him know if she approved.

Cody knew that he should just be going by what she'd told him on her deathbed, that she wanted him to move on with his life and not be alone, but that had been eight years ago. What he really needed was something more current. He wanted to be assured that it was still all right for him to marry someone else.

That he had her blessings.

Maybe he was asking for too much. Maybe he should just go and—

And then he heard it. A meadowlark. A western meadowlark, and it was singing. Renee had always loved hearing the bird's melodic tune. Whenever she'd hear it, she'd stop whatever she was doing or saying and just listen.

She used to say to him that it was a boy bird singing to his girl. He'd tease her, saying that there was no way for her to know that, but she'd remain adamant about it, certain she was right.

That was just the way she was.

Grinning as he recalled all this, Cody looked up at the sky, searching it for a sign of the meadowlark. And then he saw it. There was no mistaking the yellow throat and belly, the bold, black V at its throat. It was a meadowlark, all right.

The next moment, the bird had flown out of range, disappearing into the horizon.

But his message lingered in the air.

"Thank you, Renee," Cody whispered softly as he put his Stetson back on his head.

Catherine's heart sank as she stood in the shadow of a massive oak tree, out of sight as she observed Cody from a distance. She was too far away to hear what he was saying, but she saw the flowers and she could tell by the set of his shoulders that the tension that had been there when she'd first walked up was gone.

He'd probably confessed his transgressions with her to his wife and was asking for her forgiveness for what he'd done.

She watched his lips move. Everything about him spoke of an overwhelming sadness.

He was still in love with his wife.

Tears gathered in Catherine's eyes.

Served her right for being dumb enough to fall so hard and so quick, she chastised herself. That wasn't like her; she never reacted that fast. And because she had, she was now paying oh, so dearly for this break in her behavior.

Her heart breaking, Catherine turned and fled the cemetery. She didn't want to take a chance on Cody seeing her.

It was over.

She didn't remember finding her car or even driving back to the shop. The entire way there had been marred by tears. Tears that blurred her vision before sliding down her face.

In the grip of despair and exasperation, Catherine kept wiping the offending tears away, doing her best to stop crying.

But she couldn't.

Each tear just brought more in its wake until she felt as if she was drowning in tears. Maybe it would have been better if she had.

But she didn't drown, didn't die of heartbreak. Somehow she managed to find her way back to the shop.

Parking her vehicle behind the shop, she locked it and entered through the back door.

She turned on lights as she went through the shop. They didn't help. Nothing helped, but it would eventually. She just had to keep going until then.

Meanwhile, there was still a huge list of things for her to do and she was going to throw herself into doing them, pushing herself until she was too exhausted to think or feel, she swore silently.

Even so, for a moment, she debated leaving the closed sign just where it was. The next minute, she decided against it. She needed customers, and talking to them would get her mind off the fact that she no longer had a heart that functioned properly. It was broken into what felt like a million pieces.

Maybe more.

Flipping the sign in the window back to Open for Business, Catherine crossed back to the counter in the center of the room, retrieved her apron from the bottom shelf and slipped it over her clothing.

There was a huge amount of dusting waiting for her in the storage room. If she was lucky, she'd wind up buried under it, she thought, unable to escape the bitterness that was assaulting her from all sides, trying to get a tight hold on her.

Fighting it off no longer seemed worth it.

Nothing seemed worth it, she thought dully, feather duster in one hand, lack of energy, of enthusiasm, in the other.

This time, when the bell over the door sounded some twenty minutes later, she was hoping to see a customer coming into the shop. She was prepared to see just about anyone from the town—except for the one person who *was* coming in.

Damn, where was he when I wanted to see him? And why is he here now that I don't? Catherine silently demanded.

The next second, she could feel her stomach constricting until it felt as if it had turned itself inside out.

Had Cody come to tell her he wasn't going to be seeing her anymore?

Another man would have just allowed his actions to speak for him by avoiding all contact with her. Not exactly a difficult thing to do, seeing as how she spent most of her day at the shop.

Cody isn't like other men, remember? That's why you like him.

Liked him, she corrected with silent anger.

"Hi," Cody said, watching as Catherine moved around the counter, flitting around and not alighting anywhere. Just like those birds he'd seen driving over here. They seemed to be all over at one point, before retreating, flying off somewhere else.

"Hi," she echoed, her teeth all but clenched together, straining the word. "You came at a bad time, Cody," she informed him coolly, deliberately turning her back on him as she gathered together a stack of papers for absolutely no reason she could think of except that she needed to have something to do with her hands. "I'm really busy today."

"Good, I'll help," he offered, reaching for the stack in her hands.

She instantly pulled it back, out of his reach. "You can't," she snapped.

He didn't understand. Why was she looking so angry? And why was she acting as if she'd been bitten by a squadron of mosquitoes?

"Why?" he wanted to know, wondering what had gotten her back up like this.

"Because you can't, that's all," she insisted, doing her best to keep the heat out of her voice as well as the hurt. "This is something I have to do myself." She nodded at the papers and realized, to her dismay, that the top sheet was blank.

And that Cody had already noticed that.

"You have to decode invisible writing?" Cody guessed, amused.

The amusement faded immediately as she said, "I don't appreciate you making jokes at my expense."

Wondering what had gotten into her, Cody nonetheless backed off. "No disrespect intended," he told her. He studied her for a couple of moments in silence, then asked with concern, "You okay, Catherine?"

"Yes!" It was the first answer that came to her lips, fashioned out of complete denial. But lying had never been her thing, even if it kept things simpler right now. So, reconsidering, she didn't bother curbing her hostile tone as she snapped, "No, I'm not."

Now they were finally getting somewhere, Cody thought. "Tell me what's wrong," he encouraged.

You, you're what's wrong. You came on bigger than life and when I fell for you, you hurried back to your dead wife, the excuse you hide behind for not living your life to the fullest.

Catherine pressed her lips together, knowing she couldn't just blurt that out. Cody would think she was crazy—and maybe she was.

So instead, she said something vague that would get him to leave. "I need some time, Cody. And space," she added.

"Time and space," he repeated, as if to check that he had heard her correctly.

Or was he just making fun of her? she wondered, ready to take on a fight despite the weariness that was rapidly invading her.

"Yes." It was a struggle to keep from shouting at him. The man had taken her heart and played handball against a concrete wall with it.

He looked at her closely, trying to see beneath the layers that had suddenly popped up between them. Had he been mistaken before, thinking she was the one?

No, he didn't think so, he decided. But right now, he needed answers. "Why?" he finally asked.

Rather than give him an answer, she snapped and pleaded, "Stop asking that."

"I'm asking that because I want to understand," he told her simply.

She closed her eyes, searching for strength. Searching for the will to just keep continuing. "Just go, Cody. Please," she entreated him. "Just go," she repeated with more feeling.

Cody looked at her in silence for a long moment, considering his options. If he did what he wanted to— dragged her into his arms and kissed her until whatever it was that was wrong was right again—she could easily press charges against him.

He had no choice, he realized, but to walk away just as she wanted him to.

Maybe if he gave her this "time and space" she was

asking for, it would somehow help her clear her head and come around again. Or at least get her to the point where she could explain to him what the hell was going on with her.

Blowing out an exasperated breath, he looked at Catherine for another long, pregnant moment, then quietly said, "All right. I'll go. For now," he deliberately qualified so that she understood that this wasn't over between them.

Not by a long shot.

Without another word, he turned on his heel and walked toward the front door.

Catherine remained exactly where she was. Only her eyes moved, staring after him. She could feel her heart sinking further down with each step he tread that took him farther and farther away from her.

The very fact that Cody was going, that he listened to her rather than challenged what she was saying and then stubbornly remained here, told her that she'd been right all along.

Cody *had* gone to his wife to apologize for his "transgression," for having any sort of feelings for another woman rather than remaining faithful to her memory.

Because, if she'd been wrong in her assessment, Cody would have fought her request, fought to remain in the shop.

Moreover, he would have tried to get her to change her mind. He would have argued with her until he managed to get to the bottom of all this.

Because Cody Overton wasn't a quitter, he was the kind of man who hung in there to fight for what he wanted.

But he obviously no longer wanted her. He wanted to leave.

And he *was* leaving.

She'd given him a way out and he'd taken it.

"Nice going," Catherine murmured sarcastically to herself.

The tears came back. But this time, she didn't bother trying to wipe them away. It didn't matter.

Nothing mattered. Because she'd lost something very precious.

No, you didn't. You never had it in the first place, a voice inside her head jeered.

The tears fell harder.

Faster.

Catherine slowly walked up to the front of the store and flipped the sign back around so that it proclaimed Closed for a second time that day.

As closed as she hoped her heart would be. Once it stopped aching this way.

Chapter Sixteen

Cody shivered involuntarily as a feeling of déjà vu swept over him.

He was back at the State Fair. Back riding the same noisy carousel with its brightly painted horses.

Except that he didn't see Renee.

Where was she?

The anxiety was new, too.

It ate away at him. He couldn't shake it. Couldn't rise above the feeling.

Something was wrong.

And then he heard it, heard the laughter. For a moment, he breathed a sigh of relief. But then he listened again. The laughter was different. It didn't belong to her.

Didn't belong to Renee.

The timbere was off, but it still filled him, filled his head, filled his heart.

There was a presence with him, but that, too, wasn't Renee.

That was when he knew. The presence he felt, the woman who was suddenly beside him, riding the carousel, was Catherine.

It was Catherine riding on the painted horse beside him. Catherine whose slender hands were wrapped around the pole that was inserted into the horse's saddle. Catherine who looked at him with love in her eyes and laughter on her lips.

Catherine.

Catherine's voice resonated in his chest and in his soul at the same time. She was saying something to him, but he couldn't make it out, couldn't hear the words. Her voice became a loud buzz, devolving into a disjointed hum that rang in his ears.

The anxiety rose up again, this time to engulf him, dark and foreboding. Because, just as Renee had all those other times, Catherine began to fade away right before his eyes.

When he reached for her, to try to somehow hang on to her, Catherine only faded faster.

And as he lunged forward, grasping the empty air, she disappeared altogether.

Heartsick, Cody tried to cry out her name, but his voice was stuck in his throat, becoming just as much of a prisoner as he was in this maddening time warp that insisted on continually replaying itself in his head.

"Help me, Cody. Free me."

He could *feel* Catherine pleading for him to save her rather than actually *hear* her.

And then there was silence. Nothing but deafening silence.

He was alone.

"Catherine!" he cried. His voice came echoing back to him as he stood looking down into the mouth of the abyss. "Catherine, where are you?"

Nothing but the sound of his own voice, vibrating with panic, came back to him.

And then the darkness closed over him as well. A sickening sense of finality washed over him.

It was over.

Cody bolted upright, sweating profusely and shaking so badly he thought he would never be able to stop.

It took him several minutes to get himself under control. This latest version of his nightmare had really spooked him.

Trying to think, to piece what he could together, he had no idea what to make of this new twist. He wasn't a man who believed in omens, but this was different. This had been so vivid, so real, as if something out there was trying to tell him something.

Was it some sixth sense, warning him that Catherine was in danger?

He honestly didn't know, but he was certain of one thing. He wasn't going to have any peace until he'd reassured himself that Catherine was safe and well.

His eyes bleary, Cody switched on the lamp on the nightstand next to his bed and picked up the clock he kept there. With effort, the numbers on the clock's face came into focus.

It was almost two in the morning.

Five more hours until dawn and even *that* was really too early for him to be knocking on someone's door.

Taking a deep breath, Cody tried to reason with himself.

That lasted for exactly three minutes and gained no ground. Frustrated, he kicked off the covers and got out of bed. Adrenaline began to surge through his veins as a sense of urgency reared its head and seized him.

He couldn't make heads or tails of it, but that didn't matter.

The only thing that mattered to him at this point was seeing with his own eyes that Catherine was all right. Because if she wasn't and he'd just remained here, immobile and of no earthly use to her, Catherine would never forgive him.

Hell, *he* wouldn't forgive himself, Cody thought in exasperated anger.

It took him less than five minutes to hurry into his clothes and run down the stairs.

Once on the ground floor, he hopped from one foot, then the other, pulling his boots on while on the run. Moving even faster, he nearly forgot to close the front door behind him as he dashed to his truck.

Doubling back, he slammed it hard. The door locked itself.

At the moment, all he had was tunnel vision. He had to see Catherine with his own eyes. Nothing else mattered right now except for Catherine.

Once behind the wheel, Cody drove like a maniac, swerving from side to side to avoid creatures that used the cover of night to forage for their food.

The only reason he didn't get into an accident with another vehicle was because, at this hour, there *were* no other vehicles on the road.

It occurred to Cody that he'd probably broken some kind of a speed record getting from his ranch to the

Clifton house, but that wasn't something he could readily ask anyone to substantiate.

He could feel his breath backing up in his throat as he drew closer to her family's house. It was just a dream, he told himself, just a dream. Catherine was fine. She *had* to be.

His hands felt like ice as he clutched the steering wheel.

Pulling up in front of the tall, imposing Victorian house, he nearly strangled on the seat belt he forgot to release. Doing so, he jumped from the vehicle, taking the steps leading to the porch two at a time.

His boots resounded on the wooden, wraparound porch. Forgoing the doorbell, he knocked—pounded actually—on the front door.

"Are you home?" he called out as he pounded the door again. "Catherine, if you're all right, answer the door!"

Three minutes into his rant, the front door flew open. But instead of Catherine, Cody found himself looking down at a white-haired, slightly bleary-eyed older man in a navy blue robe thrown over a pair of light blue pajamas.

The confused scowl on the round face told Cody exactly what Amos Clifton thought of being dragged out of bed at this ungodly hour.

"What the hell is wrong with you, boy?" Amos demanded in a deep, booming voice. "You have *any* idea what time it is?"

Equally agitated and frustrated, Cody answered, "Yes, sir, I do."

"Then why the hell are you banging on my door, yelling at the top of your lungs like some drunken banshee?" He eyed Cody, not sure what to make of any of this. "You deliberately *trying* to raise the dead?"

Cody took a deep breath, standing his ground. "No, sir, what I'm trying to do is find out if Catherine's all right."

Amos's expression indicated that he thought he was talking to a lunatic. "Last I looked, she was, but that was before all this yelling and screeching started. Now she's probably hiding from the madman standing on our veranda," he predicted. He shouted a question at him, "Just what is your problem, boy?"

To be heard, Cody raised his voice as well and shouted, "I'm in love with your daughter."

White eyebrows drew together in suspicion. "That would be Catherine?" Amos asked impatiently. "Be specific. I've got more than one daughter."

"Yes, sir. Catherine, sir," Cody confirmed. Shifting nervously, Cody realized that this was going to be his moment of truth. There was no turning back from this now—not that he wanted to. "I take it that you're her father?"

"Well, I'm sure as hell not her mother," Amos retorted, wondering if Cody was dangerous or just some lovesick cowboy.

Cody took in another deep breath, silently warning himself not to hyperventilate. "Sir, I want to ask for your blessings."

"Done. You've got it. My blessings," Amos parroted. "Now will you go home?"

Determined, Cody plowed on. "I want to marry your daughter. Catherine," he added in case the man had forgotten he'd specified that earlier.

In response to his proclamation, Cody heard a round

of squeals. The noise was coming from inside the house. More precisely, from the young women gathered at the top of the stairs inside the house. Drawn by the sound of raised voices, they'd remained to listen to this exchange between their father and Catherine's suitor.

Flabbergasted, Amos stuttered, "Well, I—" Before he could finish, he was being gently pushed aside as Catherine came to the front door.

"I'll handle this, Daddy," Catherine told him, then turned to look at Cody. Part of her thought she'd just imagined this last part of the exchange between her father and Cody. "Did I hear right? Are you seriously asking me to marry you?"

Cody was at a loss as to what she was actually thinking. Her somber expression gave nothing away. It definitely wasn't what he was hoping for in response to his proposal.

"Yes," he told her emphatically.

She wanted to believe him. More than anything in the world, she wanted to believe that Cody actually wanted to marry her.

But what she'd witnessed this afternoon told her otherwise and very nearly negated his proposal. "You're still in love with your wife, Cody," Catherine told him crisply.

"Wife?" Amos echoed from inside the house. "This lunatic is married?" he demanded, growing incensed.

Catherine held up her hand, wordlessly asking for her father's silence. Her father was so stunned, he did as his oldest daughter requested. He held his tongue.

"I saw you at the cemetery yesterday," she told Cody. "Saw you standing there for a long time, talking to her."

He had no idea how Catherine came to be there, but

that wasn't the point right now. Getting her to understand why he'd gone to the cemetery was.

"I was," he confirmed. Then, before she could tell him to leave, he said, "I was saying goodbye."

"Goodbye?" Catherine repeated uncertainly.

Moving closer, Cody took her hands in his. "Yes. I was telling her that I was going to ask you to marry me." He smiled, certain now that he was doing the right thing. He could feel it in his bones. "I love you," he told her with feeling. "Ever since you fell into my arms, I've been thinking about the future. *Our* future."

"What do you mean, she fell into your arms? Fell from where?" Amos wanted to know, still not completely convinced that he didn't have a crazy man standing on his doorstep.

"I'll explain it all later, Daddy," Catherine promised, never taking her eyes off Cody. "Go on," she coaxed.

Cody shook his head, annoyed with himself. This wasn't coming out the way he'd planned. The words were all jumbled up.

"Let me start over," he said to Catherine.

Before she could protest for him to just keep going, she saw Cody getting down on one knee. Her heart began to beat faster as, still kneeling, he took one of her hands in his.

"I promise you that as long as I draw breath, you'll never know a day without my love." He paused, wanting to get the words just right. "Catherine Clifton, will you do me the incredible honor of becoming my wife?"

Stifling a shriek of joy, Catherine fell to her knees so that she could be on the same level with Cody. She threw her arms around his neck and cried, "Yes, oh, yes."

There was a chorus of cheers behind her as her sisters all ran down the stairs to be part of this joyful moment. Even her father was now beaming at the way this scene had just played itself out.

But all that Catherine would learn later. Right now, she was completely focused on the man who was able to make the entire world fade away when he kissed her.

The world was held at bay for a long, long time.

It completely astounded Catherine how incredibly quickly a wedding—with all the trimmings, yet—could be pulled together when the members of her family all worked in concert the way they did for her.

The moment she said yes and agreed to be married as soon as possible, Catherine's family went into high gear. A wedding dress was purchased and subsequently altered to meet with her delighted approval, miraculously ready the night before the wedding. The menu for the perforce large reception was decided upon before the sun set on the momentous day that had begun with such loud pounding on the family front door.

Cody even agreed to wear a modified version of a tuxedo—anything to make Catherine happy *and* his wife.

A week later, accompanied by a huge flock of butterflies that were flapping wildly and breeding at an incredible speed within the confines of her abdomen, Catherine clutched a large bouquet of pink roses as she stood beside Cody on the steps of her back porch, her sisters and brothers comprising the wedding party and standing up, grinning, behind the nervous bride and the contented groom.

Catherine truly couldn't remember *ever* being happier, despite the dive-bombing butterflies in her stomach. Funny how things managed to arrange themselves sometimes. All she'd initially wanted to do was to carve out a little independence for herself by buying the shop and turning it into a success.

She'd gotten her independence and so much more.

Though she'd thought about it a lot, she'd never thought that she would actually wind up getting married. Never thought that she could ever be as wildly in love as she was right now at this very moment.

If she was dreaming, then she never wanted to wake up.

For a split second, Catherine mentally took a step back and looked around. Everyone she'd ever cared about and loved, her family and her friends, were all gathered together to celebrate her happiness.

Their happiness, she amended, slanting a glance at the man who was several words away from becoming her husband.

It just didn't get any better than this, Catherine thought.

"And do you, Cody Overton, take Catherine Clifton for your lawful wedded wife, to love and honor, through sickness and health, for richer or poor, for better or worse, as long as you both shall live?" the minister asked.

There wasn't even a microsecond of hesitation on Cody's part. He gave his answer immediately. "I do."

"And do you, Catherine Clifton, take Cody Overton for your lawful wedding husband, for richer or poorer, for better or worse, in sickness and health, as long as you both shall live?"

The minister barely had time to finish his sentence before Catherine loudly cried, "I do."

With the rings in place and the vows taken, the minister nodded, closing the worn book he'd used for guidance for the last couple of decades. "Then, by the power vested in me by the state of Montana, I now pronounce you husband and wife. All right, you may now ki—"

The minister laughed, aborting what he was about to say. There was no need to utter those final instructions. The newlywed couple had beaten him to it.

With a chuckle, he commented, "Well, you certainly took to that like ducks to water."

His observation was met with laughter from everyone except for the bride and groom. They were otherwise occupied and intended to be so for a while longer.

Epilogue

Twilight was slowly creeping in on dusky feet outside the small, quaint bed-and-breakfast where Cody and Catherine were honeymooning.

And were officially beginning their married life together.

While it was growing darker outside, inside the room where they were staying was an entirely different matter. Catherine was fairly certain that any moment, their bed was going to ignite from the sheer heat that they were generating as they came together time and again.

Almost spent and tottering on the brink of sheer exhaustion, Catherine curled up into her husband as they lay together, waiting for the pounding of their hearts to subside to a normal rhythm.

They had been at the inn for two days and nights now and had yet to venture outside.

Cody brushed his lips against her forehead, sending yet another wave of absolute contentment sweeping through her.

"Any regrets?" he murmured.

"Just one," she answered after a moment's consideration.

Cody raised himself up on his elbow and looked at the woman who lay cradled in his arm. Her answer surprised him. Whatever was wrong, he intended to fix it.

"Oh?"

Catherine nodded and ran her hand along his cheek, the small movement testifying to the overwhelming love she felt for him.

"I regret that I didn't find my 'real vintage cowboy' years earlier," she told him, doing her best to keep a straight face.

Cody's features softened as he grinned at her. "Well, I figure we can always try to make up for lost time now," he told her.

"There is that," she agreed, turning her body into his, the very movement extending a silent, open invitation to her brand-new husband.

Cody paused for a second, overwhelmed by the realization that he was one hell of a lucky man, finding his soul mate not just once, but twice in one lifetime. What were the odds?

"Just let me catch my breath," he requested, following it up with a very sensual wink.

"I can do that," she answered, her eyes sparkling as she nodded her head.

Cody's arm tightened around her, holding Catherine closer than a prayer. "Tell me, how would you feel about having a whole bushel of little real vintage cowboys and cowgirls?" he wanted to know.

"Wonderful," she answered with enthusiasm. "I'd feel wonderful." She shifted so that she could look at Cody's face and gauge whether or not he was serious. To her delight, he was. "How soon can we get started?" she asked eagerly.

He pretended to consider the question in earnest. "Well, you know, it's a might tricky business, getting these little folks to be just right. I'd say that we're going to need some practice. Actually, lots and lots of practice," he amended.

She nodded, as if taking what he was saying seriously. "Practice, right," she agreed, adding, "Then I'm your girl."

Damn lucky, he thought again. "You most certainly are that," he responded, then said it again for reinforcement, in case she hadn't heard him the first time. "You most certainly are."

The words were barely spoken before he threw himself into the project they had both just committed themselves to. He kissed his bride long and hard.

"Work" never promised to be more exhilarating than right at this moment.

* * * * *

Look for
THE MAVERICK'S READY-MADE FAMILY
by Brenda Harlen, the next book in
MONTANA MAVERICKS: BACK IN THE SADDLE
On sale October 2012.

COMING NEXT MONTH from Harlequin®
Special Edition®

AVAILABLE SEPTEMBER 18, 2012

#2215 THE MAVERICK'S READY-MADE FAMILY
Montana Mavericks: Back in the Saddle
Brenda Harlen
Soon-to-be single mom Antonia Wright isn't looking for romance, single dad Clayton Traub only wants to make a new start with his infant son, and neither one is prepared for the attraction that sizzles between them....

#2216 A HOME FOR NOBODY'S PRINCESS
Royal Babies
Leanne Banks
What happens when a Texas nanny learns she is the biological daughter of a prince? Her rancher boss steps in to help protect her from the paparazzi, but who can protect her from her attraction to him?

#2217 CORNER-OFFICE COURTSHIP
The Camdens of Colorado
Victoria Pade
There's only one thing out of Cade Camden's reach—Nati Morrison, whose family was long ago wronged by his.

#2218 TEXAS MAGIC
Celebrations, Inc.
Nancy Robards Thompson
Caroline Coopersmith simply wanted to make it through the weekend of her bridezilla younger sister's wedding. She never intended on falling in love with best man Drew Montgomery.

#2219 DADDY IN THE MAKING
St. Valentine, Texas
Crystal Green
He'd lost most of his memories, and he was back in town to recover them. But when he met the woman who haunted his dreams, what he recovered was himself.

#2220 THE SOLDIER'S BABY BARGAIN
Home to Harbor Town
Beth Kery
Ryan fell for Faith without ever setting eyes on her. Their first night together exploded in unexpected passion. Now, he must prove not only that the baby she carries is his, but that they belong together.

You can find more information on upcoming Harlequin® titles, free excerpts and more at www.HarlequinInsideRomance.com.

HSECNM0912

REQUEST YOUR FREE BOOKS!
2 FREE NOVELS PLUS 2 FREE GIFTS!

SPECIAL EDITION
Life, Love & Family

YES! Please send me 2 FREE Harlequin® Special Edition novels and my 2 FREE gifts (gifts are worth about $10). After receiving them, if I don't wish to receive any more books, I can return the shipping statement marked "cancel." If I don't cancel, I will receive 6 brand-new novels every month and be billed just $4.49 per book in the U.S. or $5.24 per book in Canada. That's a saving of at least 14% off the cover price! It's quite a bargain! Shipping and handling is just 50¢ per book in the U.S. and 75¢ per book in Canada.* I understand that accepting the 2 free books and gifts places me under no obligation to buy anything. I can always return a shipment and cancel at any time. Even if I never buy another book, the two free books and gifts are mine to keep forever.

235/335 HDN FEGF

Name	(PLEASE PRINT)	
Address		Apt. #
City	State/Prov.	Zip/Postal Code

Signature (if under 18, a parent or guardian must sign)

Mail to the **Reader Service:**
IN U.S.A.: P.O. Box 1867, Buffalo, NY 14240-1867
IN CANADA: P.O. Box 609, Fort Erie, Ontario L2A 5X3

Not valid for current subscribers to Harlequin Special Edition books.

Want to try two free books from another line?
Call 1-800-873-8635 or visit www.ReaderService.com.

* Terms and prices subject to change without notice. Prices do not include applicable taxes. Sales tax applicable in N.Y. Canadian residents will be charged applicable taxes. Offer not valid in Quebec. This offer is limited to one order per household. All orders subject to credit approval. Credit or debit balances in a customer's account(s) may be offset by any other outstanding balance owed by or to the customer. Please allow 4 to 6 weeks for delivery. Offer available while quantities last.

SPECIAL EDITION

Life, Love and Family

Sometimes love strikes in the most unexpected circumstances...

Soon-to-be single mom Antonia Wright isn't looking
for romance, especially from a cowboy. But when
rancher and single father Clayton Traub rents a room
at Antonia's boardinghouse, Wright's Way, she isn't
prepared for the attraction that instantly sizzles between
them or the pain she sees in his big brown eyes.
Can Clay and Antonia trust their hearts and build the
family they've always dreamed of?

Don't miss

THE MAVERICK'S
READY-MADE FAMILY

by Brenda Harlen

Available this October from Harlequin® Special Edition®

*What happens when a Texas nanny learns she is
the biological daughter of a prince? Her rancher boss
steps in to help protect her from the paparazzi, but who
can protect her from her attraction to him?*

*Read on for an excerpt of
A HOME FOR NOBODY'S PRINCESS
by* USA TODAY *bestselling author Leanne Banks.*

Available October 2012

"This is out of control." Benjamin sighed. "Well, damn.
I guess I'm gonna have to be your fiancé."

Coco's jaw dropped. "What?"

"It won't be real," he said quickly, as much for himself
as for her. After the debacle of his relationship with Brooke,
the idea of an engagement nearly gave him hives. "It's just
for the sake of appearances until the insanity dies down.
This way it won't look like you're all alone and ready to have
someone take advantage of you. If someone approaches
you, then they'll have to deal with me, too."

She frowned. "I'm stronger than I seem," she said.

"I know you're strong. After what you went through for
your mom and helping Emma to settle down, I know you're
strong. But it's gotta be damn tiring to feel like you've
always got to be on guard."

Coco sighed and her shoulders slumped. "You're right
about that." She met his gaze with a wince. "Are you sure
you don't mind doing this?"

"It's just for a little while," he said. "You mentioned that
a fiancé would fix things a few minutes ago. I had to run it
through my brain. It seems like the right thing to do."

She gave a slow nod and bit her lip. "Hmm. But it would cut into your dating time."

Benjamin laughed. "That's not a big focus at the moment."

"It would be a huge relief for me," she admitted. "If you're sure you don't mind. And we'll break it off the second you feel inconvenienced."

"No problem," he said. "I'll spread the word. Should be all over the county by lunchtime. No one can know the truth. That's the only way this will work."

Coco took a deep breath and closed her eyes as if preparing to take a jump into deep water. "Okay" she said, and opened her eyes. "Let's do it."

Will Coco be able to carry out the charade?

Find out in Leanne Banks's new novel—
A HOME FOR NOBODY'S PRINCESS.

Available October 2012 from Harlequin® Special Edition®

HARLEQUIN *Blaze*™

red-hot reads

Two sizzling fairy tales with men straight from your wildest dreams...

Fan-favorite authors
Rhonda Nelson & Karen Foley
bring readers another installment of

Blazing Bedtime Stories, Volume IX

THE EQUALIZER

Modern-day righter of wrongs, Robin Sherwood is a man on a mission and will do everything necessary to see that through, especially when that means catching the eye of a fair maiden.

GOD'S GIFT TO WOMEN

Sculptor Lexi Adams decides there is no such thing as the perfect man, until she catches sight of Nikos Christakos, the sexy builder next door. She convinces herself that she only wants to sculpt him, but soon finds a cold stone statue is a poor substitute for the real deal.

Available October 2012 wherever books are sold.

HARLEQUIN® Romance

At their grandmother's request, three estranged sisters return home for Christmas to the small town of Beckett's Run. Little do they know that this family reunion will reveal long-buried secrets... and new-found love.

Discover the magic of Christmas in a brand-new Harlequin® Romance miniseries.

Holiday Miracles

In October 2012, find yourself
SNOWBOUND IN THE EARL'S CASTLE
by **Fiona Harper**

Be enchanted in November 2012 by a
SLEIGH RIDE WITH THE RANCHER
by **Donna Alward**

And be mesmerized in December 2012 by
MISTLETOE KISSES WITH THE BILLIONAIRE
by **Shirley Jump**

Available wherever books are sold.

celebrating
15 YEARS

Another heartwarming installment of

**Two sets of twins, torn apart by family secrets,
find their way home**

When big-city cop Grayson Wallace visits an elementary
school for career day, he finds his heartstrings
unexpectedly tugged by a six-year-old fatherless boy and
his widowed mother, Elise Lopez. Now he can't get the
struggling Lopezes off his mind. All he can think about
is what family means—especially after discovering
the identical twin brother he hadn't known he had
in Grasslands. Maybe a trip to ranch country is just
what he, Elise and little Cory need.

Look-Alike Lawman
by Glynna Kaye